ELIZABETH HOPKINSON is the author of *Asexual Fairy Tales* and *Asexual Myths & Tales*. She was featured in the BBC's We Are Bradford project, and was on Stonewall's first ace/aro panel.

Her short stories have appeared in *The Forgotten & the Fantastical* and *Dancing with Mr Darcy*, along with many other anthologies and magazines. Her story *A Short History of the Dream Library* won the James White Award.

Elizabeth has appeared at Leeds LGBT+ Literature Festival, Ilkley Literature Festival Fringe and Swanwick Writers' Summer School. She lives in Bradford with her husband, daughter and cat.

Elizabeth is a romantic asexual and is committed to asexual representation in fiction.

Find out more about Elizabeth at: elizabethhopkinson.uk

ANNA HOPKINSON is a 22-year-old book and children's book illustrator from Bradford. Illustrator of *Asexual Fairy Tales* and *Asexual Myths & Tales*. Find her on Instagram at @annahopkinson_art or on Twitter at @hopkinson_anna

To see more of her work, visit her website: annahopkinsonart.com

D1604017

Praise for Elizabeth Hopkinson

"We always have a huge demand for asexual themed books, but sadly there's just not that many good titles around at the moment. Both *Asexual Myths & Tales* and *Asexual Fairy Tales* by Elizabeth Hopkinson sell really well for us and we've had amazing feedback from our customers for both of them. We literally can't wait to read the latest Ace stories from Elizabeth."

— Jason Guy, Director of Gay Pride Shop, Manchester

"We are SO excited to hear of a new collection of Asexual Tales from Elizabeth – the first two have been a huge success for the bookshop. When there is still so little asexual representation in print it's really thrilling as booksellers to be able to offer brilliantly written and produced titles offering just that to our readers – we will always welcome more!"

— Mairi (she/her), Lighthouse - Edinburgh's Radical Bookshop

"These Asexual Fairy Tales sound like old folk tales, perfect for reading out loud. More than just a retelling or adaptation, Elizabeth has succeeded in creating something new without losing that old-world storyteller feel."

— Jaylee James, editor of *Circuits and Slippers*

"Fairy tales are a part of every child's life. As we grow up, we learn mythology, history, and legends. Yet, for asexuals, the representation has always been rare to non-existent. What Elizabeth Hopkinson has done is brought aces to the forefront in these pieces of writing. It's an incredible and necessary thing! Everyone wants to see a character that is like themselves in what they read or watch, even when it comes to fairy tales. So what Elizabeth is doing here is greatly appreciated, and we wish her the very best!"

— Kelsey Lee, Social Media Director of AVEN

More Asexual Fairy Tales

Elizabeth Hopkinson

Illustrated by Anna Hopkinson

SilverWood

Published in 2022 by SilverWood Books

SilverWood Books Ltd
14 Small Street, Bristol, BS1 1DE, United Kingdom
www.silverwoodbooks.co.uk

Copyright © Elizabeth Hopkinson 2022
Images © Anna Hopkinson 2022

ISBN 978-1-80042-228-5 (paperback)

British Library Cataloguing in Publication Data
A CIP catalogue record for this book is available from the British Library

Page design and typesetting by SilverWood Books

For you

Contents

From the Author

What is an asexual fairy tale? If you haven't read the first two books, you might well be asking yourself this question. And the answer you give yourself might not be the same as mine.

I'm a heteroromantic apothisexual. (Very much yes to romance; very much no to the sexual act). I'm greygender (partially relating to a gender outside the binary) and see that as part of my asexual identity. I'm also a wife and mother. I didn't identify until my late 30s, and am now in my late 40s. I'm a Christian; I belong to a dispersed religious community, inspired by Celtic monasticism. I have long term medical conditions: depression/anxiety and fibromyalgia. I have a degree in English Language and Literature, and see myself as an amateur fairy tale scholar.

Why am I telling you this? Well, because asexuality is a very broad spectrum of identity that intersects with many other aspects of identity. No two aces are going to see the world - or being ace - in the same way. So, although I try to be sensitive to other aces in my storytelling, I can only truly represent myself. I know that can be frustrating because there is still so little ace representation in the world. But I hope you will find things here that you can relate to, whether you are asexual or not.

The stories in this book are a combination of retold tales from around the world and my own, original stories. All of them have what I believe to be ace-coded (and sometimes nonbinary-coded) representation.

Apart from "Ash" (which is a gender-swapped Cinderella) I haven't altered the source tales to make them asexual or nonbinary. I've just retold them in a way that brings out the asexual symbolism I see in them. A wife whose head detaches in bed. A man who thinks he's made of glass. These things speak to me at the level of the deep soul. Where several stories or folkloric beliefs from different cultures seem to chime in with one another, but aren't close enough to be the same story, I've combined them to make a new story. Wholly original tales like "Paper Prince" are an attempt to express the soul-deep realities of my life in symbolic language. Which is what all myths, legends and folktales have

11

done from time immemorial.

I hope you enjoy the tales in this book as much as I have enjoyed telling them. And I hope you enjoy Anna's exquisite illustrations. They really are something special.

I exist and I am proud.

Elizabeth Hopkinson,
May 2022

The Story of Amethyst

1

The Story of Amethyst

'Amethyst' is one of my favourite words. It has such a beautiful sound. This story sounds as if it ought to be a classical myth, but it actually comes from a poem about precious stones: Les amours et nouveaux échanges des pierres précieuses *(1586) by the French Renaissance poet Rémy Belleau. I couldn't resist the idea of the purple in the asexual flag having its own origin myth.*

A woman named Amethystos was travelling to the Temple of Diana in the Sacred Grove, deep in the heart of a forest. She was going there to worship the inviolate goddess because she wished to remain untouched. Coupling was not for her.

Unfortunately, the forest was also home to Bacchus, god of wine, who was not known for his temperate behaviour. Even when sober, he was not one to restrain his appetites. And he was seldom sober.

"Lovely lady, why are you worshipping Diana? Surely you're not still a virgin at your age?"

Amethystos quickened her pace.

"You just need to have a drink and relax. You'll soon lose your inhibitions."

Amethystos knew he was talking rubbish. And she knew her best defence was speed. She began to run. Under the boughs, over the roots, through the undergrowth.

Bacchus followed. Through the undergrowth, over the roots, under the boughs. But Amethystos was fleet of foot, and a drunk doesn't make the best runner. Bacchus was soon tripping over roots, and getting twigs entangled in his long ringlets. Amethystos was getting away. So he released his tigers: two huge guardian beasts who lay at either side of his forest throne when he tasted his finest vintage. At a word from Bacchus, they sprang forward like two fiery comets. Graceful. And deadly.

Amethystos knew they were pursuing her, but she daren't look back. A moment's hesitation could cost her the advantage. Lose that and she would soon feel hot breath on her heels. And then...what?

She ran as fast as she could. Branches snagged the sleeves of her dress. Branches of gold. She had crossed the border of the Sacred Grove. She was within Diana's realm. "Diana, help me!" she prayed.

Immediately, she felt her body change. Her limbs became heavy, her movements slower. Soon she had no limbs at all. What was left of her grew harder, fused together. Amethystos knew that she was strong. Strong and beautiful, in a way that let the light through. Though she could no longer speak, she *shone*.

By the time Bacchus reached the grove, there was no woman, no Amethystos. Only the goddess Diana, and a transparent gemstone of unusual beauty.

"What happened here?" he said.

Diana's eyes narrowed. "I always protect my own."

Bacchus sank to his knees. "I'm a drunken fool, aren't I?"

Diana said nothing.

"Allow me to make an offering in penitence." Bacchus took a flask from his hip and poured wine over the gemstone. The colour seeped into its crystalline structure, turning it an ethereal purple.

"I accept your offering," said Diana, "in lieu of the one Amethystos would have made. But don't think this means you've got to her. On the contrary, from now on the gemstone called the amethyst will be proof against drunkenness, with the ability to neuter the effects of wine. Not only that, it will calm all physical passions, and be known as the gemstone of spirituality."

Her prophecy came true. For many centuries, the amethyst was carried by those who wished to remain sober, or to sense a calming of the spirit. But then something happened that Diana did not foresee. The clear violet of amethyst joined with the white of marble, the silver-grey of the moon, and the black of ebony to become a symbol that would bring pride and identity to many. The asexual flag.

Guigemar

2

Guigemar

'Guigemar' is a Breton lai (a story in verse) told by medieval poet Marie de France in the late twelfth century. (The same author wrote 'Bisclavret', which is retold in Asexual Myths & Tales.)

In medieval symbolism, a wound to the thigh is associated with impotence. (For example, in Arthurian legend the Fisher King's wound causes barrenness in the land, and interestingly can only be cured by the virgin knight Sir Galahad.) The white deer is a symbol of androgyny.

I think it's interesting that Guigemar's 'other half' is a woman in a tower; an inviolate like himself. (She has no name in the original; I named her Rossignol, or 'Nightingale', after one of the other Breton lais.) In the original text, it is explicit that their relationship becomes sexual. I didn't want to imply that sex is necessary, but I wanted to make it clear that not all aces are sex-averse romantics like me, so I left open the possibility. The story of Guigemar and Rossignol can mean whatever you want it to mean.

In Brittany, there was once a knight, the son of a baron, named Guigemar. He was everything a knight should be: handsome and brave, noble and kind. Everyone loved him. But Nature had made him differently to the other knights around him. He had not the slightest interest in love. Many a woman would happily have had him as a husband or a lover. But no matter what advances they made towards him, he showed no response.

One day, Guigemar was out hunting in the forest. His beaters ran ahead of him, and a servant carried his bow, quiver and hunting knife. The hounds soon caught the scent of a stag, and Guigemar quickened the pace of his steed.

The dogs bayed. A deer ran out from the cover of a bush. But it was a deer like none Guigemar had ever seen. Its coat was pure white. It had the antlers of a stag, yet it suckled its fawn like a hind.

Regardless of the wonder of the encounter, Guigemar bent his bow. The arrow struck the deer in the forehead, but rebounded, wounding Guigemar in the thigh. He tumbled from his horse onto the thick grass.

The deer spoke in a voice that was neither male nor female. "Alas, I am mortally wounded. But you, Sir Knight, shall share my fate. That wound in your thigh will never be cured by potion or herb. It can only be cured by the love of a woman, who will suffer for you as you suffer for love of her."

Hearing this, Guigemar knew he was doomed. For he had never been touched by love, not once in his life. In pain and shame, he remounted and rode away from the scene, allowing no servant to follow him.

A green path led him out of the wood and into an open space. A cliff dropped away from the plain, and a creek lay at the foot of it. There was a harbour, where a single ship lay at anchor. All its timbers were of ebony, and its sail was of silk. Guigemar had never heard of a harbour in these parts. But he dismounted and, in great pain, boarded the ship. He'd expected to find sailors there, but there were none. Instead, there was something he had not expected. A four-poster bed stood in the centre of the ship. It was made of cypress and inlaid with gold. A quilt of silk and gold thread lay upon it, with a coverlet of sable fur. The pillows were soft. In pain, Guigemar eased himself onto the bed. The moment he did so, the ship set sail. There was no chance for Guigemar to disembark. He would have to go wherever the ship took him.

In an ancient city not far from that place lived a lady named Rossignol. She was kept imprisoned in a castle keep, with a thick wall on one side and the sea on the other. A maid-in-waiting and an old eunuch priest were her only companions. She had been locked in the keep by a jealous husband old enough to be her grandfather. He was unable to consummate the marriage, but lived in a jealous agony lest another man steal his treasure. So he kept Rossignol under lock and key, though he visited her but seldom.

The keep where she lived comprised a chapel below and a bedchamber above. The walls of this chamber were covered in paintings of Venus, goddess of love in her divine aspect, instructing young wives in obedience. In the central panel, the goddess cast Ovid's *Ars amatoria* into the fire. A caption engraved beneath it warned of excommunication to any who dared read this ancient handbook on the arts of love, or try what it recommended.

Such treatment by her husband left Rossignol confused. She had never been in love, much less felt desire for a man. How was she expected to be ignorant of love's arts and still please her husband? How was she meant to never think of a man, and then to think of her husband above all the moment she became a wife? What was love, anyway?

Early one afternoon, Rossignol was walking in the garden by the shoreline with her maid, when they saw a ship rising on the waves and coming into harbour. They could not understand how it was being sailed, as there was no crew to be seen. The maid, who was the bolder of the two, took off her surcoat, waded out to the ship and climbed aboard. There she saw no other soul but Guigemar, lying pale upon the bed. She felt sure he was dead. But if she should be mistaken... Returning to her mistress, she told what she had seen.

"We should bring him ashore," said Rossignol. "If he is dead, we can bury him. Our priest can help. If he is alive, we might nurse him back to health."

"Come and see him, mistress," said the maid.

When Rossignol beheld Guigemar lying on the bed, she wept. It grieved her that such a handsome knight should lose his life so young. She placed a hand upon his chest. A heartbeat! The knight was alive!

Guigemar opened his eyes. "Where am I?" he said.

They told one another their stories. He, how he had been wounded. She, how she was kept imprisoned in this keep.

"If you wish to stay until you are fit to travel, we will gladly shelter you," she said.

Guigemar thanked his rescuers. They helped him to his feet and, with some difficulty, supported him as they made their way to the keep. On reaching the bedchamber, they settled Guigemar in the maid's bed, behind a curtain that divided the room in two. They brought a golden basin of water to wash his wound, wiping away the blood with white linen, then binding it tightly. When the priest brought supper, they saved a goodly portion for Guigemar, who ate gratefully.

Over the next few weeks, Rossignol and her maid nursed Guigemar, and he became stronger. His appetite increased and he was able to get out of bed. And he noticed something strange. The wound in his thigh no longer ached. But how could that be? The white deer had told him that the wound could only be cured when he was loved to the point of suffering, and suffered love in return.

Rossignol felt warmth growing in her heart. Could this be love? It was nothing like the dutiful depictions of Venus in the paintings, nor the knowing arts of Ovid. But she truly cared for Guigemar as she had for no one else. "Could this sweet ache I feel in my heart be love?" she asked him.

"I know not," Guigemar replied. "I know only that my wound has ceased to bleed, and I have a new, pleasurable pain that I think only you could assuage."

As for what the lovers did – or did not do – next, I will leave it for the reader to decide. For there are some who, though they have never felt attraction in that way, will yet join bodies with one they trust. There are others for whom bodies have no part in romantic love. And yet others for whom Venus is anathema, yet they love their friends to the death. Let the reader believe, then, that Rossignol and Guigemar pledged their love in whatever way seemed right to them.

I have said that Rossignol's husband visited her but seldom. Yet she could not avoid him forever. From time to time he would visit the lonely castle keep, fumbling ineffectually at his pretty young wife, while she bit back her tears. As his health improved, Guigemar, hidden behind the curtain, found these visits all the more frustrating. He longed to rescue Rossignol from her tormentor, and once or twice made movements towards the curtain that almost betrayed his presence.

At last, Rossignol said, "If you stay here any longer, you will be discovered. We must part. God grant that we are reunited in the future! But to protect ourselves in the meantime, let us create chastity belts for ourselves."

So saying, she took the tailpiece of Guigemar's shirt and tied it about his loins, fastening it with a knot that could not be undone except by her. Guigemar did the same thing for Rossignol, girding her with a sash that none but he could unfasten.

The very next day, Rossignol's fears came true. A chamberlain sent by her husband came knocking upon the door of the chamber. When they would not open to him, he fetched three men to break it down. Guigemar stood, unafraid, and seized a fir-wood pole used for hanging clothes. He was determined to defend himself. Seeing the danger, the chamberlain questioned him. Guigemar explained all about the hind and the wound, and how the young lady had nursed him back to health.

"A likely tale!" the chamberlain said. "If it's true, where is your ship?"

"Out there," Guigemar pointed.

The chamberlain hauled him outside, and there was the ship, just as Guigemar had said. "Get aboard, then. And don't come back to this country again!"

Guigemar did as he was told. The ship set sail, back to his home country. He wept and sighed all the way, praying for death if he could not see Rossignol again.

He did not die, however. The ship put into harbour in the exact spot from which it had embarked a year and a half ago. Guigemar was met by a knight and squire who recognised him and took him to his home. His friends were overjoyed that he had been found, but Guigemar was downcast. Although he was urged many times to take a wife, he said he would only marry the lady who could undo the knot in his shirt. Over the following months, this news carried throughout Brittany, and many a lady came to make the attempt, only to depart unsuccessful.

But what of Rossignol? On the advice of the chamberlain, her husband imprisoned her in a tower of black marble, even more impregnable than the first. There she suffered for two years, mourning and praying that she might find Guigemar once more. One day, she could take it no longer.

"Oh, Guigemar, why did we ever meet?" she sobbed. "Let me escape this place or let me die!"

In desperation, she seized the massive handle of the door. It turned, and the door opened.

Her prayers were answered! There in the harbour lay the magical ship. Rossignol climbed aboard and the ship set sail, pitching on the waves with such force that it flung her onto the deck.

The ship reached port in Brittany, beneath a fine, strong castle belonging to a certain Lord Meriaduc. This lord was waging war on his neighbour, and had risen early to send forth his troops. Looking from the castle window, he saw the ship below and went down with his chamberlain to inspect it. They climbed the ladder and stepped onto the deck, only to find that the only soul aboard was a lady as lovely as a fairy!

Meriaduc was delighted by his discovery. He bore Rossignol off to his castle, where he lodged her with his younger sister in a fine chamber. There she was served and honoured, richly attired, but she remained downcast. Many times, Meriaduc asked for her hand in marriage, but she refused. She would only marry the man who could untie the true-love knot in her sash.

When Meriaduc heard this, he became angry. "Why are young people acting so strangely nowadays? There is a knight of renown in this country who says the exact same thing. He will marry no one but the lady who can undo the knot in his shirt. I should knock your two heads together!"

At this news, Rossignol swooned and almost lost consciousness. Meriaduc cut the lacing of her tunic and tried to untie the knot, but he could not. Afterwards, many knights were summoned to make the attempt on Meriaduc's behalf, but none of them could do it.

Things continued in this manner until Meriaduc at last prepared to go to war. He summoned knights to fight for his cause, Guigemar among them. Guigemar arrived in his finest clothes and armour, with more than a hundred knights under his command. Once he was inside the castle, Meriaduc arranged for his sister to come and greet Guigemar in the tower where he was lodged. Of course, Rossignol came with her.

When the two lovers saw one another, both grew pale. Rossignol only stayed upright by clinging on to Meriaduc's sister.

Guigemar's mind was in a frenzy of torment. Can it really be her, after all this time? She looks like my beloved Rossignol. But I have imagined her so many times. Could my eyes be deceiving me? Kneeling, he kissed her hand and offered her a seat. He could not manage a word.

Meriaduc gave a feigned laugh. "Lord, if you wish it, this lady will attempt to undo the knot in your shirt."

Guigemar blushed to the roots of his hair. But he bared himself sufficiently for the knot to be seen. Rossignol trembled and did nothing. She hardly dared believe her senses.

Guigemar spoke in a choked voice. "Please, My Lady. Try to undo it."

With a deft touch, Rossignol untied the knot as easily as she might have taken the pin from her hair. "And now, Sir Knight, you must undo the knot in *my* belt," she said.

She bared it. Guigemar knelt and untied it in one smooth movement. Tears ran down both their cheeks.

"Beloved, take your sweetheart away," Rossignol pleaded.

Guigemar got to his feet. "My Lord," he said to Meriaduc, "I have this day discovered a friend whom I had thought lost forever. Allow me to take her home with me. In return for this favour I will serve Your Lordship three years, and put a hundred knights at your disposal."

Meriaduc's eyes narrowed. "Not done," he said. "Now you have kindly removed the chastity belt, the lady is mine."

"We put those chastity belts there ourselves, to protect us from people like you," said Guigemar. "If you will not allow us to leave in peace, I must issue a challenge. My knights against yours."

Meriaduc agreed to the challenge. That very day, Guigemar departed with his knights and made for the stronghold of Meriaduc's enemy, who was only too happy to have such a large force join his cause. The next day they rose early and made a noisy exit from the town, hooves clattering and trumpets blaring. They besieged Meriaduc's castle until the townsfolk surrendered. The unscrupulous lord was defeated and lost his life.

Guigemar and Rossignol were reunited once more. Together they left for Guigemar's home, where they lived a long and happy life together. And on the anniversary of their homecoming, folk often claimed to have seen a white hind with the antlers of a stag pause in a clearing of the forest, then turn and walk away.

The Marzipan Husband

3

The Marzipan Husband

This story comes from The Tale of Tales *or* Pentamerone *(1634–6), a Neapolitan collection of fairy tales by Giambattista Basile, which contains early versions of 'Rapunzel', 'Cinderella' and 'Sleeping Beauty'. Basile's telling is called 'Pinto Smauto' ('Painted Enamel'). There is also a Greek version called 'Mr Simigdáli' ('Mr Semolina'). It's a variation on the myth of Pygmalion (retold in the first* Asexual Fairy Tales*), only with confectionery. I know not everyone likes marzipan but I love it! And yes, I may have played a little on the 'aces prefer cake' stereotype in this one. And made a passing reference to Korean palace dramas...*

B etta dreamed of romance. Violins and rose petals. Frost and starlight. Mysterious kingdoms under the sea. She dreamed of walking arm in arm through a woodland glade, with a young man pretty enough to be her sister. She imagined standing at the altar as a bride; parting curtains of white lace to reveal the bridal bed. Then holding a bonny baby in her arms. As for what came in between, she could not picture it. And she certainly never dreamt of what her father had in mind.

"Why aren't you engaged yet? You should have a young man at your age."

Betta opened and shut her mouth. As if it was that easy! Boys just weren't attracted to her. They found her too good, or too childlike, or... She didn't know. Sometimes she thought she was in love, but when she saw couples kissing like they were suctioned together, she thought she couldn't be. Because she didn't want to do *that*.

But her father was very sure of what *he* wanted. "I've arranged some dinner dates for you with the most eligible men in the neighbourhood. Choose one."

Betta hated those suitors. They terrified her. A huntsman with a beard and hairy hands. A baron's son with a square chin and a seductive smile. A musketeer with a chest like a rack of oars. "I'm sorry," she told them one by one. "I can't accept your proposal. Thanks for dessert, though." She really did like dessert. Had love's pleasures consisted of almond croissants and tiramisu, there would have been nothing to fear.

And that gave her an idea. "Father, next time you go to market, can you pick up some things for me?"

"Be better if you picked up a husband," her father grumbled.

"This will get me a husband." Betta gave him her best smile. "If you can get me a sack of ground almonds and one of sugar, a bottle of rose water and a pinch of cinnamon. Oh, and some decorations, please. Gold leaf, if they have it, forty pearls, two sapphires, and a few garnets and rubies."

Her father's eyes bulged.

"They don't have to be genuine," Betta laughed. "As long as they look pretty. And don't forget a bowl and a silver scalpel."

"Oh. Right." Her father didn't know what to make of this request. But if it would get his daughter a husband, he was prepared to go along with it. He returned from the market with everything Betta had asked for.

Betta took it all to her room and mixed a huge quantity of marzipan. The sweet almond scent was divine! She flavoured it further with the cinnamon and rose water, then began to sculpt a life-sized man from the mixture. She made him as beautiful as if he'd just come from a Korean palace: slender and smooth with high cheekbones. His eyes were sapphires, his teeth pearls, and his cheeks blushed red with rubies and garnets. Betta kissed the youth on his marzipan lips, licked away the crumbs of sugared almond and swallowed them. Oh, heaven! Then she prayed to the goddess of love. "Bring him to life, as you once did with Galatea, the maid of marble. May this youth be as sweet in temper as marzipan and rose water."

The sculpted figure blinked his eyes, yawned and stretched. There before Betta was the man of her dreams. He took her by the hand and kissed it delicately. "Thank you, Betta, for bringing me to life. I am yours, if you will be mine."

Betta could hardly speak. It had worked. She gave the young man an awkward hug, and took him downstairs to meet her father. "Father, this is my betrothed husband. We just got engaged. His name is...er... Marchpane[1]."

Her father looked towards the door of her room and scratched his head. He had not seen a youth go in, yet one had come out. Being a simple man, he put two and two together and made five. If a suitor had climbed in through his daughter's window to enjoy secret time together, that was fine. He had the result he wanted: his daughter would be married at last.

It was a wedding of unusual splendour. A marquee was erected in the street, with a fountain of milk and another of wine. People came from near and far to pay their respects to the bride and her father, who was as proud as a peacock on that day. They also came to see if the rumours were true; if Betta had indeed found herself a husband of exquisite beauty. It was whispered that he was one of the fey, or an ancient god returned to earth.

One of the wedding guests was the queen of a small country bordering Betta's own. She was a collector of objets d'art. Her home was filled with glass butterflies, jewelled eggs, enamelled boxes, and automata that played the harpsichord or wrote letters in ink. When she saw Marchpane, a covetous spirit rose within her. "A bejewelled man with hair of gold! I simply must have him for my collection." Sidling up to Marchpane, she offered him a glass of wine. "Congratulations, Signor, on your nuptial day. I wonder, do you enjoy a pretty sight? I have a golden coach, cunningly crafted to resemble a ship, and six white horses to pull it, with the horns of narwhals on their headdress. Would you like to see? It's just around the corner."

Poor Marchpane had not existed in this world long enough to understand its wiles. He was as innocent as a child, and that's no surprise since he was born of Betta's imagination. He followed the queen to her coach, and was easily persuaded to sit inside. Immediately, the queen commanded her coachman to drive, which he did, with the speed of a squall.

Circulating among the wedding guests, Betta did not immediately

[1]   An old-fashioned word for marzipan

notice that her husband was missing. But when she began to search, she could find him nowhere. Not in the marquee, nor by the fountain of milk. Not in the terrace garden, nor on the balcony, nor in any room of the house. At last someone volunteered that they had seen him being handed into a coach, which had left in a hurry. Betta could come to only one conclusion. Marchpane had been kidnapped.

She put out word to the watchmen, who had the town crier give out a notice, with a reward for any information leading to the return of Marchpane. But no one knew a thing, except that he had left in a golden coach made to look like a ship. This one clue was Betta's only hope. She packed a few essentials and set off in search of her missing husband.

She hadn't gone far when she began to feel unwell. Her breasts ached and her stomach turned sour. The second time she vomited, she thought she had better seek help. So she turned aside for the cottage of an old hedge witch who was known for her knowledge of women's ailments.

"Your problem is obvious," said the witch. "If indeed it *is* a problem. The fact is, you're pregnant."

"Impossible!" Betta said. "I haven't... I mean, that's why I made myself a husband of marzipan. So I wouldn't have to..."

The witch scratched her chin. "I think we'd better have this from the beginning."

Betta explained.

"I see," said the witch. "And did you eat any of the marzipan?"

"Well, I licked my lips," said Betta. "You know, after we kissed."

The witch snapped her fingers. "There you have it, then. A marzipan baby is growing inside you."

"As simple as that?" Betta asked.

The witch shrugged. "Apparently."

Betta heaved a sigh and sank to the cottage floor. "Thank God! Another prayer answered."

The hedge witch proved remarkably helpful. Not only did she give Betta food and shelter – and a tonic for morning sickness – but she taught her three powerful charms. "You may need these along the road you travel," she said. "For the world is a dangerous place. But only use them when in great need. Once spoken, they cannot be used again."

Betta thanked the old witch and continued on her journey.

After many months, she arrived in a new land, at a city called Round Mountain. This was the summer residence of that country's queen, a queen who had this year brought home with her a beautiful young man with eyes of sapphire and hair of gold. A man who left the scent of almonds and rose water in his wake. *Marchpane.* It had to be him. But how to get access to him? The summer palace was guarded on all sides and surrounded by a fence topped with golden spears.

Betta rubbed her aching back. "I suppose I'm too far gone to ask for a job." She didn't know how long a marzipan child took to grow, but her belly was now quite large. "Perhaps someone will take pity on me, though." She smeared mud on her cheeks and ripped at the small holes where her petticoats had caught on thorns. Then she went swooning to the back gate of the palace. "For mercy's sake, a drink of water and a seat! I'm a poor, pregnant woman with nowhere to go."

This brought all manner of servants rushing out, from stable boys to scullery maids. They sat Betta on a three-legged stool and placed a horn beaker of milk in her hand.

"You poor thing," said the cook, who had daughters of her own. "You can't go wandering the world like that. We'll make you up a bed of straw in the stable, and I dare say you can do a little mending while you're waiting for the child to arrive."

Betta thanked her, and was soon installed in her new lodgings. From there, she found subtle ways to sneak around the grounds, and it wasn't long before she glimpsed Marchpane, standing on a balcony and looking out over the valley. Her heart rattled against her ribcage. He was here! She'd found him. But how to get him away from the queen without being pursued by a hundred guardsmen? Now, if ever, was the time to use the witch's charms.

Betta uttered the first spell and before her there appeared a miniature golden carriage encrusted with jewels. It moved by clockwork, the horses trotting and the coachman flicking his whip. When the queen's ladies-in-waiting saw the glint of gold in the gardens, they soon came running to see what it was, and then they went to tell the queen.

"I must have it for my collection," the queen said. "Tell the girl to bring it here. I'll pay any price."

But Betta wasn't stupid. "Tell the queen that I'll only part with it

33

if Her Majesty allows me one night in the chamber of the man with sapphire eyes."

Now, when the queen had first kidnapped Marchpane, she had intended to use him as a concubine. But Marchpane was as innocent as a child when it came to matters of the bedroom. Moreover, when she had stripped him, the queen had found that he lacked the necessary equipment. And no wonder, for he had been born of Betta's imagination. So now the queen thought, let the silly girl have her wish. She'll soon taste bitter disappointment. But on second thought she decided that she couldn't bear to have other people touching her things, so, on the night in question, she slipped Marchpane a sleeping draught so he would lie like a log until morning.

When Betta entered the bedchamber, she found Marchpane already sound asleep. She shook him and called his name. "Marchpane, wake up! I've come such a long way to find you. The queen tricked you and stole you away. I'm your wife, and I'm having your marzipan child." But it was no use. Betta talked herself hoarse, but Marchpane did not wake.

She did not allow herself to be defeated, though. After she had been escorted back to her stable, she decided to try the second charm. She said the words of the spell and there appeared a golden cage with a jewelled nightingale inside. The little bird sang any tune you asked it to sing.

Of course, the queen soon got to know of this. "Tell the girl to bring it. I must have it for my collection," she said.

Betta's reply was the same as before. "The price is one night spent in the chamber of the man with sapphire eyes."

The queen played the same trick as before. Marchpane slept like a log, and nothing Betta said could rouse him.

However, the next morning when Marchpane awoke, he decided to go for a stroll in the gardens. He wished he could walk further, but every time he tried to leave the palace grounds, twenty guards surrounded him. He'd thought of mounting an escape but, truth to tell, he was afraid of being kidnapped again, or attacked. He didn't exactly blend into a crowd, and people might take his bejewelled appearance as an invitation to theft. He wished he was back with Betta – though he had known her for such a short time, he felt like he had been made to love her. Those days felt like a dream to him now; he was starting to doubt that they had ever happened.

As he was walking, not looking where he went, he collided with a stable boy who was fetching water from the well. After helping the boy to his feet and apologising, Marchpane asked why the boy was in such a hurry. "I don't normally see you at this time of day," he said.

"I overslept and must rush to catch up," said the boy. "It's that pregnant beggarwoman who sleeps in the stable. She's been up at the palace for the last two nights. Then she comes back in the early hours, crying and cursing about her poor, lost husband. 'The queen must have drugged him,' she says. That's why she couldn't wake him. Funny thing is, I could have sworn she said your name, Signor. You haven't had a woman in your chamber, have you?"

"I couldn't say," Marchpane answered. "The last two nights, I've slept..." Like a log. "Where is this beggarwoman now?"

But at that moment, along came the guards, and Marchpane was escorted back to the palace. He made up his mind, though, not to drink anything the queen offered him that night. He would pretend to drink, then pour it away. He had to know what was going on.

Meanwhile, Betta was close to despair. She only had one charm left, and then she would be out of ideas. Doubtless, Marchpane would be drugged again tonight, but what else could she do?

She said the third spell. This time, bolts of silk spilled all over the stable floor. Blushing apricot, vivid blue, ivory shot through with caramel. Sashes embroidered with golden seashells. Blush pink sewn with tiny seed pearls.

It wasn't long before the queen sent word. "Tell the girl to bring the cloth. I must have it for my collection. Only think what a fabulous wardrobe I will have!"

"Her Majesty knows the price," came Betta's reply. "One night in the chamber of the man with sapphire eyes."

This time, when Betta came to his chamber, Marchpane was slumbering only lightly. She shook his shoulders as usual and called his name.

"Marchpane! Marchpane, wake up! I've come such a long way to find you. The queen tricked you and stole you away. It's Betta, your wife. I'm having your marzipan child."

Marchpane blinked and opened his eyes. "Betta, is that really you?" It was hard to believe that this travel-worn woman with straw in her hair and a pregnant belly was the same Betta who had kissed him to life in her father's house.

"Yes, Marchpane, it's really me." And she told him the whole story: about the marzipan pregnancy, the hedge witch and her charms, and the marvels she had traded for three nights in his chamber. "And now we must escape, my love. The queen shan't keep you a moment longer."

Marchpane was unsure how they were going to manage that. But he said, "First you must take back your magical gifts. It's only just that, after the suffering she's caused, we hit the queen where it really hurts: in her treasure hoard."

The treasures were housed in the chamber next to Marchpane's – for of course, the queen liked to keep all her precious possessions in one place.

Marchpane picked up a strongbox of coins and a casket of jewels. "She owes us these as interest," he said. He was no longer quite so naive as he had once been.

Betta turned to retrieve the magical objects. As soon as she touched them, they came to life and helped the pair escape. The nightingale flew them out of the window on her back. The carriage – now life-sized – carried them away to safety. And the silken cloths transformed into clouds that screened the escaping couple from view.

Using the queen's money, Betta and Marchpane rented a smart little lodging where their baby was born. He looked just like his father, with sapphire eyes and a scent of almonds. But he had Betta's smile.

Eventually, when Betta had recovered from the birth, they returned to her father, who was overjoyed to see his daughter and son-in-law alive, and more thrilled than I can say to have a new grandson. In fact, he was so pleased to have an heir to the family business that he never questioned the fact that there were now two marzipan people living in his house.

Betta and Marchpane got along as if they had been made for each other (which was half true, of course). Their married life never again contained as much romance and adventure as it had started out with, but it never had so many tears, either. And when, in time, they felt the need for another child, all Betta had to do was kiss a little bit of marzipan from Marchpane's lips.

The Clockwork Bride

4

The Clockwork Bride

This is an amalgam of three stories. The first is a Russian tale, 'Prince Danila Govorila', which appears in Aleksandr Nikolaevich's Russian Folk-Tales (1916), and again in Jen Campbell's The Sister Who Ate Her Brothers *(2021), where it appears as 'The Kingdoms at the Centre of the Earth'. Since the older version includes Baba Yaga as a character, I added some details from other Baba Yaga stories.*

The second is 'A Toy Princess' (1877) by Victorian fairy tale writer Mary De Morgan, retold by Kate Forsyth in Vasilisa the Wise and Other Tales of Brave Young Women *(2017). Interestingly, Marilyn Pemberton writes on the website of the De Morgan Collection that there is 'no evidence' of Mary having had 'any romantic relationships'.*

The third is the ballet Coppélia *(first presented at the Théâtre Impérial de l'Opéra, Paris, on 25 May 1870; subtitled* The Girl with Enamel Eyes*), and the Gothic tale that inspired it, 'The Sandman' (1817) by E T A Hoffmann (which also inspired* The Nutcracker*).*

All three source tales involve a girl or woman being replaced by a doll. I didn't want this to turn into a tawdry tale about sex toys, but I did want to highlight the wish to be both present with and absent from one's partner, and the tension that brings; and to ask, "What is 'natural'?"

I gave a lot of thought to the issue of whether to keep the threatened brother–sister marriage we find in 'Prince Danila Govorila'. Actually, real or threatened incest is found in a lot of myths and folk tales, maybe as a way of dealing with trauma (notably Aarne-Thompson-Uther Type 510B 'Donkeyskin', in which father–daughter marriage is threatened). The last thing I want to do is trigger traumatic memories in my readers, and I hope I have handled the matter with sensitivity. But the story also taps into a Jungian archetype in which the sibling prefigures the future partner. Before

I identified as ace, I struggled to differentiate between the feelings I had for a lover and those for a brother. As a young person this caused me a lot of worry, even to the point of fearing that I was incestuous because I couldn't tell the difference. Now that I understand that my love for any boy was asexual, I can see the cause of my confusion more clearly. But it was real at the time. I could have used a story like this.

There once was an aged queen who feared that her son, Prince Daniel, would never find a bride. So she went to the witch Baba Yaga, who gave her a ring set with a blue enamel stone.

"Tell him to marry whomever this ring fits," she told the queen.

So Prince Daniel travelled all around the kingdom, trying the ring on the fingers of eligible young women. But it fit none of them. Eventually he came home and showed the ring to his sister, whose name was Ursula. "I'm fed up of this wretched ring!" he said. "Why won't it fit anyone?"

Princess Ursula turned the ring around in her hands. "I've no idea," she said, and slipped the ring onto her finger. It fitted perfectly.

"Why did I not think of this before?" Daniel cried. "Look at your eyes! Just like blue enamel. *You* shall be my bride!"

Now, Ursula was very fond of her brother Daniel, and had secretly wished that they could run away and live together. But not as husband and wife! "You don't mean that," she said. "You can't."

But he did.

Ursula ran to her room and took out a wooden doll that had been left to her by her grandmother, the dowager queen. "If ever you're in trouble," the dowager had said, "feed a little bread and milk to the doll and tell her your worries. It will help and guide you."

So Ursula fed a crumb of white bread and a silver thimbleful of milk to her grandmother's doll, and told it her troubles.

The doll opened its little black eyes and blinked twice. Then it opened its little rosy mouth and spoke. "Don't fear, Ursula, dear. I will help you. Now, let me out at your window, and I promise to come back before your wedding night."

The princess did as the doll asked, and it went clattering away on its little wooden feet until it came to a street that only cats could find, hidden in the space between two terraced houses. There stood the workshop of Dr Coppélius, maker of mechanical marvels.

"Good day to you, Doctor," said the doll. "I need you to make me a marvel, and have it done by Prince Daniel's wedding day."

"Good day to you too, Matryoshka," said Coppélius. "What sort of marvel do you require?"

"A clockwork princess," the doll replied, "in the exact likeness of Princess Ursula."

"A walking, talking princess, finished by the royal wedding day?" Dr Coppélius scratched his beard. "It'll cost you."

"How much?"

"Four cats' footfalls, three fishes' screams and two swans' songs."

"Done," said the doll. "Have it delivered to the palace on the night of the wedding."

On the wedding night, just as promised, the doll was waiting for Ursula in the bridal chamber.

"Are you nearly ready, Ursula?" Daniel called.

"One moment! I'm just taking off my earrings," Ursula replied. She turned to the doll. "Where were you all that time? He could come in at any minute!"

"Don't fear, Ursula, dear," said the doll. "Just open my little belly and we'll see what happens."

Ursula opened the doll's round, wooden belly, and out came three more dolls, all exactly alike. They stood in the four corners of the room and began to sing.

"Are you ready, my love?" Daniel called.

"I'm just unfastening my girdle," Ursula called back.

The four dolls sang:

Cuckoo! Cuckoo! At Prince Daniel's command.
Cuckoo! Cuckoo! Princess Ursula takes his hand.
Cuckoo! Cuckoo! Now his sister's his wife.
Cuckoo! Cuckoo! Now a doll comes to life.

"Are you ready now?" Daniel called.

"Nearly. I'm just taking off my shoes," Ursula replied.

The dolls sang on. And as they did so, a crack began to open in the chamber floor.

Cuckoo! Cuckoo! Now his sister's his wife.
Cuckoo! Cuckoo! Now a doll comes to life.
Cuckoo! Cuckoo! Now the earth opens wide.
Cuckoo! Cuckoo! Ursula, fall inside!

And with a scream, Ursula fell through the crack and plummeted into the earth.

Daniel broke down the chamber door. "What is going on in here?"

But the dolls carried on singing. "Cuckoo! Cuckoo!"

"Shut up! Stop singing that!" He reached for his sword.

"What on earth are you doing?" said a voice behind him. "They're only my childhood dolls that Grandmother gave me. You wind them up and they make that sound, like a cuckoo clock."

Daniel blinked. Of course; how silly of him.

"Are you coming to bed?" said his bride. She smiled at him. Her eyes were blue enamel.

Ursula fell down and down and down, through fire and water, through earth and air, until she landed with a bump in a gloomy forest where there stood a hut on chicken legs, surrounded by a fence of bones.

Sitting in the open doorway of the hut was a fair maiden, knitting with gold and silver thread. When she saw Ursula, she leapt to her feet and ran to give her a hug. "Sister! I've been waiting so long for you to come."

"I don't have a sister," Ursula began to say. But the words *I have a brother* stuck in her throat. She didn't want to think about that.

The maiden just grinned. "But I know you are the sister I've been waiting for all my life. My name's Swanilda."

Swanilda invited Ursula into the hut and showed her what she was working on. As a princess, Ursula had never had to work, but she very much wanted to be able to turn thread into clothes. It was like magic!

"Will you teach me how to knit?" she asked Swanilda.

"Of course, but we must be careful," Swanilda said. "My mother is Baba Yaga, the witch. If she finds you here, she will eat you!"

Ursula's eyes widened.

"But don't fear, Ursula, dear. When the time comes, I will hide you."

So they sat side by side, and Swanilda taught Ursula how to knit. The time passed by very pleasantly. Too soon, however, the hour drew near when Baba Yaga would return home. Swanilda turned Ursula into a twig, and hid her in the witch's broom.

Baba Yaga came in, sniffing. "Why does this house smell of human blood?"

"Oh, some soldiers came by and asked for a drink of water. But they were too tough for your old teeth, so I let them pass by."

Thus Swanilda tricked the witch. And the next day, she and Ursula once again knitted and chatted together, becoming more friendly by the minute. When it was time for Baba Yaga to come home, Swanilda turned Ursula into a twig once more, and hid her in the witch's broom.

Baba Yaga came in, sniffing. "Why does this house smell of human blood?"

"Oh, some old men came by and asked for a bite to eat. But they were too shrivelled for your old teeth, so I let them pass by."

The next day passed as before. By now, the two girls were firm friends. Ursula felt that Swanilda was her sister indeed.

"We should run away together," she said. "Get away from your terrible mother."

"Good idea," said Swanilda, and they began to make plans.

They were so busy planning that they didn't notice Baba Yaga come home.

"Oho!" she cried, licking her lips. "Not a soldier, nor an old man, but a delicious young princess for me to eat!" And she tried to push Ursula into the oven on a shovel.

But Ursula stuck out her feet against the walls of the hearth. However hard the witch pushed, she could not get her into the oven.

"Ah! You will wear me out!" Baba Yaga said, and collapsed onto the floor.

Instantly, the two girls seized her and pushed her into the oven instead. Then they snatched up their knitting, a comb and a brush, and fled. But Baba Yaga is not easily destroyed. She came flying after the fugitives in her giant mortar, powered by her pestle.

"Throw down the brush!" Swanilda yelled.

Ursula threw it down and it became a dense thicket of bushes. Baba Yaga was forced to stop when she reached it. But she scratched through it with her clawlike nails, and pursued them once more.

"Throw down the comb!" Swanilda yelled.

The comb became a forest of oak trees. Baba Yaga was forced to stop. But she gnawed at it with her iron teeth, and pursued them once more.

"There's nothing else for it. Throw down the knitting!" Swanilda yelled.

Ursula threw down the gold-and-silver knitting. In its place sprang up a great lake of fire. The flames burnt Baba Yaga to a crisp, and that was the end of her.

The girls stood gasping, staring at the charred remains.

"Where do we go now?" said Swanilda.

Ursula took her hand. "I don't know. But we'll go there one step at a time."

In the meantime, Daniel was very pleased with the bride he thought was Ursula. She sang and played the piano beautifully, with a voice like chiming glass bells. She danced with perfect timing, never getting the steps wrong or treading on anyone's toes. When he wanted to talk to her, she sat quietly and listened, not busying her hands with distracting embroidery or knitting, as some girls did. She never argued with his plans. And when he wanted to make love to her, she was perfectly responsive, saying only, "Ah! Ah!"

Then came a day when she seemed unwell. Her movements became slow and jerky; her speech slurred. Finally, there came a terrible grinding and twanging noise from inside her belly, and her head flopped onto her chest. The prince sent at once for doctors to examine her. They came back with grave news.

"Your Highness is the victim of some cruel trick. The princess is not a living woman. She is just a clockwork doll." And they showed him his bride with her head removed. The body was a metal shell of cogs, wires and levers. On her motionless hand sat the ring with the blue enamel stone. "The marriage must be annulled," the doctors said. "Your Highness must take a proper, human wife."

Daniel held the doll's head in his hands. Her blue enamel eyes stared back at him, unblinking. "But she was so perfect," he said. "So perfect."

Meanwhile, Ursula and Swanilda walked on, hand in hand, into the fresh green land of a new beginning.

Mistress and Maid

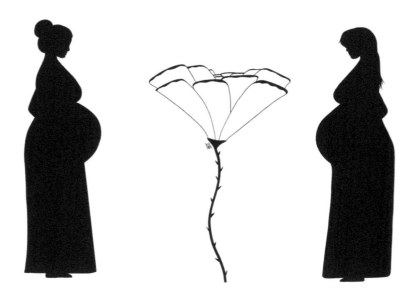

5

Mistress and Maid

This brief tale is drawn from three sources: 'The Enchanted Doe' from The
Tale of Tales *(see 'The Marzipan Husband'), 'Ghvthisvari (I am of God)'
from* Georgian Folk Tales *(1894) by Marjory Wardrop, and* The Passion
of Saints Perpetua and Felicity, *a text concerning third-century North
African Christian martyrs who died in Carthage (modern-day Tunisia).
There are remarkable similarities between these very different stories, all of
which involve a mistress and a maid giving birth together, and two of which
deal with my pet theme of parthenogenesis. It's good to write a story that
celebrates female friendship and brave mothers.*

There once lived a noblewoman and her maidservant who – in
spite of their difference in status – loved each other as though
they had but a single heart between them. The two women
had secretly converted to a forbidden religion. When their secret was
discovered, the noblewoman was cut off from her family and housed in
a tower in the middle of the sea, so that her treachery could not bring
shame upon her family. And the maidservant went with her.

One day, the women looked at the sea and saw a strange fruit
floating towards them. It looked like a glass apple of purple and blue.

"It is the food of the Sea People," the maidservant said. And she
fished it out of the sea with her hairnet.

The fruit looked delicious. The women cut it in two and ate half
each, enjoying its sweet, wild taste. Strange to say, as soon as the fruit
was eaten, both women became pregnant, and theirs were no normal
pregnancies! Their bellies swelled up quickly, and in a few days, each
had given birth to a baby boy. The boys grew just as rapidly, growing as

much in a day as a normal child does in a year. When they reached the age of sixteen, their growth slowed and they began to age at the same rate as everyone else. They were the very image of each other; as alike as twins. Only their mothers could tell them apart.

The mothers knew that their lives were in danger. So they said to the boys, "We love you dearly, but you cannot stay here. Call for your father, the sea, to take you away to a new land. We will not forget you."

So the two boys stood on the shore and called for the sea. At once, a mighty wave arose. With a cry of farewell, the boys dived in and were swept away to a new land, where they began adventures of their own. Many tales have been told of their valour and their loyalty to one another. But this is not their tale. This tale tells of their mothers.

Their pregnancies had not gone unnoticed. A fisherman had seen the boys' strange growth, and he reported it to the noblewoman's family. Their retribution was swift. Surely these were witches! The family would shelter them no longer. The women were turned over to the authorities for their forbidden practices, and sentenced to death by wild beasts. As they sat in the common prison, surrounded by the other convicts, they prayed for deliverance.

That night, the noblewoman had a dream. She was being led out into the arena to face a gladiator of monstrous size. As she stepped out, she transformed into a man: a warrior. She fought the giant and he fell, defeated, at her feet.

"Everything will be all right," she told the maidservant in the morning. "We will conquer."

The next night, the maidservant too had a dream. She dreamt of a ladder leading from the arena into the clouds. At the bottom was a poisonous snake. The maidservant stamped on the snake, then she and her mistress climbed the ladder and escaped to a country far away.

"Yes, everything will be all right," she told the noblewoman the following morning. "We will rise above this."

The next day was the day of their execution. They were led out into the arena to face a maddened cow; its udders heavy with milk; its horns sharp and twisted.

"Be brave," said the maidservant to her mistress.

"You too," the noblewoman replied.

They hugged one another and kissed once. Their two hearts beat as one.

As the cow's trampling hooves approached, the crowd gasped in shock. The women had vanished. In the spot where they had embraced, a flower was growing. A rose with a red heart, and petals of pure white lined with pink.

The Golden Nugget

6

The Golden Nugget

This is a traditional Chinese tale celebrating platonic love between friends.
It was recorded by Norman Hinsdale Pitman in A Chinese Wonder Book
(1919).

Gold is easy to gain; a true friend is harder to find. True friends each see the colour of the other's soul, and love it as their own. Never let anyone tell you that such soul-friendship is inferior to other kinds of love. On the contrary, it is love of the very highest degree. It can never be broken by wealth or by poverty.

Ki-wu and Pao-shu were two such friends. On the streets of the city, the two young men were a familiar sight, walking together shoulder to shoulder, laughing and chatting as they made their way towards the teahouse, or skating along the frozen river in winter, racing one another. But today was a spring day – a holiday – and the friends had escaped the city with its dust and noise. They were climbing the winding path towards the pine forest. Birds called from the trees, and all the colours looked fresh and new, as if they'd just been painted.

Ki-wu took a deep breath. "Just smell that forest air! This is the life!"

Pao-shu laughed. "When we get beneath the trees, I'm just going to lie down on the grass and breathe in all this green. I've been working so hard lately in the shop. My master doesn't give me a minute's rest. 'Fetch this, Pao-shu! Weigh that, Pao-shu!' Stick a broom up my rear and I'll sweep the floor as I go!"

They both laughed again.

"And I've been studying so hard for my exams." Ki-wu yawned. "I see texts from the Confucian Classics floating before my eyes when I lie in bed."

"Then let's enjoy ourselves while we can," said Pao-shu.

They crossed a stream and headed deeper into the woodland. Flowers bloomed on the forest floor, stippling it with pinks and yellows and dreamy blues. Their perfume mingled with the fresh smell of damp earth. It made the friends feel gloriously alive.

"Let's go this way," said Pao-shu, as they came to a fork in the path. "We can sit on the rocks by the spring. It'll be lovely and cool."

But before they had gone much further, they spotted something lying in their path. Something yellow and shiny, about the size of a lemon. A gold nugget.

"Where did that come from?" said Pao-shu. "It must be a gift from the forest spirits."

"A gift?"

"Yes, my friend. A gift for you!" Pao-shu exclaimed. "To reward you for all your hard study."

"No, no." Ki-wu wagged his finger. "If anyone deserves a gift, it's you."

Pao-shu took a step back. "Nonsense. You've worked so hard, Ki-wu."

"Ah, but," Ki-wu assumed the manner of his tutor, "don't the great masters say that study is its own reward?" He grinned. "Come on, Pao-shu. It's got to be yours. Just think. You could leave your master and buy your own shop. Imagine that!"

They joked back and forth for a while, each insisting that the other take the nugget. At last, they began to laugh.

"This is ridiculous! Let's just leave the stupid thing where we found it."

"Exactly. We came here for trees, not gold."

"Nothing's worth arguing and losing our friendship over."

So they dropped the gold nugget back onto the path and, with their arms around each other's shoulders, headed in the direction of the spring. But when they got there, they found that they were not alone. A field labourer was stretched out by the water, fast asleep with his hat over his eyes.

"Let's move him on," Pao-shu whispered. He prodded the sleeping man with his toe. "Hey, friend, do you want to get rich? There's a gold nugget back there, just lying on the path for anyone to take."

"What?" The man sat up and rubbed his eyes.

Ki-wu repeated what Pao-shu had just said, and described exactly where the nugget was. The man scampered away at speed.

Pao-shu grinned. "Good luck to him." He sat on the rocks and took off his shoes. "And now we have the place to ourselves. I'm going to bathe my feet in the water."

Ki-wu sat beside him, and they laughed and chatted happily, talking of their hopes and ambitions for the future.

Suddenly, the labourer returned. "What sort of trick do you think you're playing on me, young masters? I could have been killed."

"What's the matter?" they said together.

"You know perfectly well," the man growled. "Telling me there was a lump of gold on the path, right where a snake was coiled, waiting. If I hadn't had my scythe on me, I would have been dead. Luckily, I'd just sharpened it. Chopped the thing clean in half."

The friends' eyes widened.

"What...?" Pao-shu began to say.

But the man was already striding away, back towards the fields.

"I don't believe this," said Ki-wu. "A snake, right where the gold was?"

"It must have been a monster, to scare the poor chap like that."

"And he cut it clean in half?"

In an instant, both were on their feet. "Let's go and see!"

Side by side, they raced back to the spot where they had found the gold. But when they got there, there was no severed snake in their path, but two nuggets of gold! Each was as large and heavy as the nugget they had discovered earlier that day. The friends looked at one another.

"Now I know for sure that Heaven has rewarded you, my friend," said Ki-wu.

"Yes," said Pao-shu, "by giving me a second chance to ensure that you get your just deserts."

And, laughing, each picked up a golden nugget and walked back to the city.

Ash, or the Gowns from a Tree

7

Ash, or the Gowns from a Tree

Strictly speaking, this isn't an asexual story, but it is a sweet, romantic fairy tale about identity. It first appeared on the Fairytalez website, where it was the winner of their Best Gender Swap Fairy Tale contest. I'm sure you'll recognise which classic fairy tale it's based upon.

There once was a boy who wished for a ball gown. His name was Ash, and he thought himself the ugliest creature in the world. He hated his clothes, his hair, the shape of his body. Whenever he caught sight of himself in a shiny kettle or the water in the well, his stomach would turn sour and he would run away. He was named for the ash tree under which his mother was buried, but whenever he spoke his own name, all he could picture were dirty sweepings from the fire.

So when he saw his stepmother and sisters getting ready for the Three-Day Ball, he balled his fists until his fingernails dug grooves into his palms. If only I were a girl and could wear a ball gown, he thought, I would be beautiful, too. Then he went and sat beneath his mother's tree, weeping angry tears.

The ball, you see, was for women only. The king was worried about his son. The crown prince had flatly refused to marry all the princesses, landgravines, infantas and dauphines the country's allies had sent. So, he had invited every eligible woman in the kingdom – and their chaperones – with the instruction that the prince must choose a bride from among them by the end of the three days. Meanwhile, the prince was miserable. How could he tell his father that no woman on earth would be right for him? His heart simply wasn't made that way.

Under his mother's tree, Ash watched the sky turn from pink to purple. "Mother, if only I had a ball gown, I could go to the palace and dance. And, just for one night, I would be beautiful."

To his astonishment, there came a creaking, cracking sound, and a door opened in the trunk of the tree. When Ash looked in, there was a ball gown of silver and white lace, with silver slippers to match. He held the gown against his body. Dare he? Before he could change his mind, he took the gown and slippers, and hurried to his sisters' room. There, before their looking glass, he changed into the marvellous gown. He brushed his hair and arranged it high with combs and ribbons. He whitened his face with powder and rouged his lips into a perfect rosebud. Then he hailed a sedan chair and headed for the ball.

The prince could not believe his eyes when Ash curtsied before him. How was it that a woman was stirring up these impossible feelings? There was a fluttering in his heart that was completely new. "May I have this dance?" The prince bowed.

Ash blushed and curtsied again, then held out his arms in elegant style as the prince whirled him about the floor. He couldn't speak. He had never felt so beautiful. Then he caught sight of himself in one of the ballroom mirrors. He was no beauty. He was Ash in a dress. The prince would see through his disguise at any moment, and despise him. "Excuse me," he mouthed, and fled the ball.

"Who was she?" was all Ash's sisters would say when they got home.

"The most beautiful woman at the ball, without doubt. The silver gown, those beautiful slippers!"

"The prince smiled at her as he did at no one else. Did you see them dancing?"

"I wonder why she ran away?"

The most beautiful woman at the ball? Ash rumpled his hair to hide his blushes. Perhaps he could go again tonight? He would go back to his mother's tree.

The prince's heart rose to his throat when he saw his partner of the previous night in an even more marvellous gown of gold embroidered with turtle doves, and walking in golden slippers. "Who are you?" he whispered in Ash's ear as they waltzed in each other's arms. "You're unlike any woman I've met."

"My name is Ash." Ash tried to lighten his voice, but he saw the prince's eyes widen, then soften.

"Perhaps you're not a woman at all," the prince said mischievously.

"I have to go." Ash gathered up his skirts and fled the ball.

But he couldn't stop thinking about the prince. To return to the ball was to risk exposing his secret, being subjected to public shame. Surely that was worse than being ugly? Yet he couldn't help remembering the prince's smile, the touch of his hand. The prince liked him. But did he only like the illusion in the ball gown, or would he like Ash for who he really was? There was only one way to find out.

"You came back." The prince held Ash gently in his arms as they whirled beneath the chandeliers. "Look, I've guessed your secret, but I haven't told you mine. I don't love women. I love... I think I love *you*, Ash. But I'd like to see your other face. If you'll allow me."

"I have to go," said Ash, but this time the prince grabbed hold of his arm. "But I'm ugly," Ash protested.

The prince shook his head. "Let me be the judge of that. But honestly, Ash, I don't think anything about you could be ugly. Please. This could be my only chance of happiness. Maybe yours, too."

Could he refuse the crown prince? Ash was starting to believe that this man had already touched his heart. "Very well, then. What should I do?"

The prince smiled. "There's a closet just through that door where they keep the footmen's uniforms. Take one and go out into the rose garden to change. It's really private there. You could drop your slippers to help me find you."

Ash took a deep breath. "Right, then. I'm going."

When the prince saw the handsome man in a blue uniform sitting among the rose bushes, his heart skipped a beat. Ash's face was still powdered and rouged – very aristocratic – and he had tied his hair back into a queue with one of the ribbons.

"There you are!" The prince beamed.

Ash stood, head bowed, fiddling with the lace on his cuffs.

Before he could help himself, the prince leaned over and kissed him softly on the cheek. "You look wonderful," he said.

"Really?" Ash raised his eyes.

"Really. In fact, I think I prefer you like this. But if you prefer a dress...?"

"I don't know what I prefer yet. Except, perhaps..." Ash cleared his throat. "Perhaps you."

The prince kissed him again, then held up Ash's discarded slippers. They glittered like frost, or glass. "I love these, by the way. Are those real diamonds?"

"I don't know," said Ash. "They came from my mother's tree. It's magic."

"So are you, Ash," the prince said.

Baillé and Aillinn

8

Baillé and Aillinn

I've always been a sucker for a good unrequited or unconsummated love story. I'm sure it's part of my ace identity.

This is a traditional Irish tale featuring Aengus, god of the Tuatha Dé Danann and hero of his own bittersweet love story. I used two sources: Brendan Nolan's retelling in Irish Love Stories *(2016) and W B Yeats's verse of 1903.*

Can you undo your destiny? Can you rewrite a prophecy? Are you destined to be loveless unless you force yourself into the mould of the majority? Or can you change the rules and do things in your own unique way?

Baillé and Aillinn were lovers in ancient Ireland. But not in the conventional way. He was a prince of Ulster; she a princess of Leinster. They loved from a distance, sending each other poetry and songs as sweet as honey. When Aillinn read Baillé's words, she felt that they described her own soul. When Baillé sang Aillinn's songs, it was like he'd been given a voice for the first time.

The time came when both determined that they should meet. They wanted to be together forever. But there was a problem. An ancient prophecy had been spoken over them both: *Baillé and Aillinn will never meet. Aillinn and Baillé will never marry.* And you can't undo a prophecy. Can you? They decided to risk it anyway. They chose Ros na Righ for their meeting place; a spot that lay at an equal distance from both their homes. There they would be handfasted, so that none might separate them.

Baillé set out first. A party of warriors rode beside him. Their cloaks of blue and green were clasped with gold brooches, and their spears were like a thicket of saplings. Alongside them rode harpers, who played and sang Aillinn's songs, accompanied by the muffled clop of their horses' hooves on the soft forest track.

"Who goes there?" the vanguard suddenly cried.

An old man was running towards the party. His ragged hair was the colour of grass, and his knees stuck out of his hose. But his eyes were as keen as a squirrel's. "Which one is Prince Baillé?" he said, and when Baillé rode forward, he went on. "My Lord, you must turn back. Your plot is discovered and the men of Leinster ride against you."

Baillé's heart turned to stone. "Where is Princess Aillinn?"

"Alas, My Lord, her father decreed that she should wed a man of her own people, not run off with an Ulster prince to share poetry. She set out to meet you but his bannermen caught up with her and surrounded her. One of the young warriors – who has always desired her, I believe – dared to take her hand and kiss it. 'My Lady, you shall wed me,' he said, 'and bed me, according to custom.'"

"How dare he?" Baillé bristled. Aillinn would be frightened and disgusted by such a suggestion. *He* would be frightened and disgusted by such a suggestion. His horse snorted and sidestepped, unnerved by Baillé's anger and distress.

The old messenger trembled. "There is worse news to come. When Princess Aillinn heard those words, her heart burst and she fell down dead."

"No!" Baillé cried. The blood drained from his face and he swayed in the saddle.

His bodyguard turned to the messenger for any word that could soften the bitter blow. But the old man was nowhere to be seen. Meanwhile, Baillé slipped from his horse and fell to the ground. His warriors clustered round him. They slapped his cheeks and put water to his lips. One felt for his pulse; there was none. Desperate, the man put his mouth to Baillé's and tried to breathe life into him. But it was no use. Baillé was cold and still. His sorrowing warriors laid him to rest upon green boughs, and buried him beneath a cairn of stones by the sea. Many a battle-hardened man wept that day, and watered the grave of Prince Baillé of Ulster.

*

But what became of the old messenger with the grass-coloured hair? He was running across Leinster, in less time than it would have taken an eagle to fly there. He made straight for the fortress of King Lughaidh, where Aillinn was even now braiding her hair and belting her cloak, readying herself for the journey to Ros na Righ. Aillinn alive? Yes, indeed. It looks like someone in this story has lied or is mistaken. And right now, that person looks very much like the old man with the ragged cloak and his knees poking through his hose.

He ran up the stairs to Aillinn's chamber and burst in without so much as knocking. The maids who were preparing themselves to ride with Aillinn yelled in surprise.

"Forgive my hasty appearance, but I bring grave news," the old man gasped. "Am I addressing Aillinn, daughter of Lughaidh?"

"I am she," Aillinn said. But she struggled to keep her voice steady. There was something in the old man's squirrel-like eyes that spoke of doom.

"Then I regret to tell you that Prince Baillé of Ulster is dead."

Aillinn's hand closed around a fistful of skirt. "Are you sure?"

"I'm afraid so, My Lady. I have just come from Dundealgin, where I saw men building a cairn of stones over a newly dug grave. When they were done, one carved in ogham letters on an upright stone, *Here lies Baillé of the house of Rudraige, who died on this spot as he rode to meet Aillinn, daughter of Lughaidh.*"

With that, the messenger turned on his heel and left the chamber. Not one word of comfort did he utter. Not that words would have done much good. Aillinn was already sinking into the arms of her maids. Her eyes became glassy, her hands cold. She was dead.

What kind of story is this, you may ask? Two loving friends tricked to death, to fulfil the terms of an ancient prophecy? Two young people punished for daring to live and love differently?

But all is not as it seems. Follow the decrepit messenger as he runs to the highest point of the hill fort, the wind rippling the grass beneath his feet. Look up and see two swans flying towards him, linked by a golden chain. They alight beside him on the grass and his body is changed. White wings sprout from his shoulders. His neck grows long and graceful. And as the sun sets in a golden glow, three swans take flight into the rosy sky.

You see, Aengus, god of love and poetry, could not bear to see Baillé and Aillinn parted. But he could not undo the prophecy either. So he took them to where the prophecy did not hold sway: the Land of Eternal Youth, far beyond the gates of death. There, they may taste the silver apples of the moon and the golden apples of the sun. There, at the doorway to the east, are three trees of purple glass which sing their own songs of such exquisite beauty that it would bring tears to your eyes just to hear them.

But is that a real marriage? Was there no sign on earth to say that Baillé and Aillinn could be together after all; that there are other kinds of marriage than the conventional sort? Wait just a little longer. The story is not over.

From the cairn where Baillé was buried, there grew a yew tree. And from the grave of Aillinn, an apple tree. These two trees grew much faster than is usual, and in seven years, each had grown so large that they were felled, and their wood used to make poets' tablets. On the yew tablet were written all the love songs of Ulster, dating from over many years, and on the applewood tablet were written all the love songs of Leinster.

Two hundred years passed. And in the second century of Our Lord, the High King of all Ireland called a gathering of all poets and storytellers at the great Hill of Tara. This gathering took place at the feast of Samhain, that marks the opening of the gates of winter. It is a time to honour the dead; a time when we may glimpse the Otherworld beyond our own, that place to which Baillé and Aillinn once flew with Aengus. Many were the poets who graced this gathering, and many were the tablets that were presented to Art, the High King, that all might marvel at the wonder of the tales inscribed upon them. And among those tablets were the yew tablet of Ulster, grown from the tomb of Baillé, and the applewood tablet of Leinster, sprung from Aillinn's grave.

King Art held the two tablets in his hands, tracing the worn ogham marks with his fingers, marvelling at the ancient tale of the two lovers doomed never to meet.

"Whose words do you judge the finer, My King?" the poet of Leinster asked nervously.

"You have many fine tales before you, to be sure," said the poet of Ulster, who could not keep a tone of pride from his voice.

But before the king could answer, the two tablets sprang towards each other and stuck fast. And try as they might, neither the king, nor his warriors, nor any of the poets could separate them. For there was another prophecy, of which no one knew; a prophecy with roots so ancient that none could have heard it spoken. Except Aengus, perhaps.

Though Baillé and Aillinn will never marry on earth, they will meet again after death, and they will never be parted.

Poetry to poetry. Song to song. Just as they had always wanted.

The Glass Lawyer

9

The Glass Lawyer

Dating from 1613, this story comes from the pen of Miguel de Cervantes, the author of Don Quixote. *What is interesting about it is that, although the story is fictitious, a condition known as 'glass delusion' was documented from the Middle Ages to the nineteenth century. Sufferers included King Charles VI of France (1368–1422; reigned 1380–1422), who had a suit of iron ribs made to protect himself, and Princess Alexandra of Bavaria (1826–1875), who believed she had swallowed a glass piano. Commentators suggest that this condition was linked to notions of purity and chastity. Alexandra never married; she became the abbess of a religious community and an author in her own right.*

In Salamanca there was once a lawyer by the name of Tomás Rodaja. He had been orphaned as a boy and adopted by two gentlemen of letters, who had paid for his education and taken him with them to visit the many sights of Europe. Tomás was a studious boy, and on returning to Salamanca had qualified as a doctor of law. He was considered a wise person by his neighbours and fellow lawyers; quick to observe and measured in his judgements. But he was not known to have ever been in love.

"He loves life," said his friends, "and people in general. What better sort of man can there be? The same cannot be said of everyone."

At that time in Salamanca there was also a beautiful lady, whose arrival had caused quite a stir among the menfolk. She was said to be witty and well travelled, having been in Flanders and Italy.

"Perhaps I met her on my travels," Tomás said. "I should go and pay my respects to her. It would not do to snub an acquaintance."

Duly, he went along to a party at the lady's house, and as soon as they met, she fell violently in love with him and became determined to have him for herself. All that night, she followed him about the room. If he made a joke, she was at his elbow, laughing too loudly. When they sat down to eat, there she was, making eyes at Tomás and sitting uncomfortably close.

"Excuse me, I have to leave," he said. He got up and left the party.

The lady was confused by Tomás's behaviour. Usually, eligible men threw themselves in her path. She had never before had someone ignore her. "Perhaps he's shy," she told herself. "I must try harder."

She tried wearing low-cut dresses. Tomás asked if she was too cold. She tried gesturing with her fan. He asked if she was too hot. She tried a more direct approach.

"You know that the man who accepts my hand in marriage will be fabulously wealthy," she said, and she smiled at Tomás from behind long, curling lashes.

Tomás turned pale. Soon he began to find excuses to avoid her. She just didn't seem to grasp that he would never feel that kind of desire for her. "I have to study," he would say, when friends proposed a visit to the lady's house. Or, "I've sprained my ankle", when there was a public ball.

She tried sending poetry. Fruit. Jewelled inkstands. He sent them all back.

The lady became frustrated. The idea that a man could refuse her was unthinkable. If I can't snare him by ordinary means, she thought, I must resort to magic.

Now, in the town was a certain wise woman, well known for her brews and potions. The lady visited this woman and asked for a love potion. "Only, can you hide it in something? A piece of fruit, perhaps?"

"Certainly. I shall inject a small quantity into a quince. That should do the trick," the wise woman said.

The next time there was a public banquet, the lady gave the quince to a servant, and told him to make certain Tomás ate it. She then watched from a distance. Sure enough, Tomás ate the quince.

The lady plumped up her lips. Now, she thought, one glance at me and he will fall madly in love.

But Tomás did not fall in love. Instead, he fell to the floor, shaking and sweating.

"He's been poisoned!" someone shouted. "Quickly! Get him to his bed and call a physician."

Tomás lay ill for many months. His body was reduced to a skeleton and he could barely speak two words together. His two fathers feared for his life. One of them began an investigation into the poisoning, but the scorned lady had already decided that a change of scenery would be wise, and left Salamanca for good. Meanwhile, physicians tried every remedy they could think of, while kindly neighbours nursed Tomás day and night.

Eventually, he grew strong enough to leave his bed. His friends and neighbours were delighted to see him up and about. They hoped he would soon begin practising law again. But his illness had brought about a strange delusion. He believed he was made of glass.

The first anyone knew of it was when his fathers saw him standing for the first time in months. One of them rushed to embrace him, but Tomás recoiled and screamed.

"Don't touch me! If you do, I'll shatter into a thousand pieces."

Naturally, the kindly soul was hurt by this outcry. But when his other father asked what was the meaning of this, Tomás replied, "I'm made of glass from head to foot. Can't you see?"

His fathers consulted the physicians, but there was nothing they could do. Nor could anyone else in Salamanca. However much they tried to persuade him otherwise, Tomás insisted he was made of glass.

Some of his friends grew impatient with this change in him. "Of course you're not made of glass. I'll prove it to you," they said. And with that, they threw themselves on Tomás and hugged him hard. "See, you're not broken. You're fine."

But Tomás screamed and shook so hard that he passed out. After that, his fathers and physicians insisted that everyone stay five paces away from him at all times. Tomás himself sent for a tailor and a blacksmith, and had them make him a suit of iron bands, which fitted over several layers of cotton wrapping. Only when wearing this did he feel safe to go outdoors. He no longer rode a horse, for fear of falling, and when he walked down the street, he always kept to the middle in case a roof tile fell on his head. In summer, he slept outdoors on the grass. In winter, he slept in the stable, buried in a pile of straw.

Most people treated him kindly, but there are always ignorant folk who make a jest of other people's misfortunes. It wasn't long before groups of lads followed Tomás around the streets, taunting him and calling him 'Dr Glasscase'. Some of them threw stones, "to see if he really smashes to pieces". You can imagine how distressing this was for poor Tomás, who really feared that the stones would shatter him.

But many in Salamanca had come to respect him since his misfortune. His lawyer's mind hadn't left him, you see. He always had a quick reply for those who mocked him, and soon he became known for his witty and insightful sayings. People would seek him out whenever they had a question, and were generally pleased with his answers. "You know, since I am made of glass, I see things more clearly," he would say. And it really did seem as if that was the case.

Soon, the fame of Tomás Rodaja spread to other towns. He began to travel more widely again. But when he did so, he always had himself placed in a packing case with plenty of straw, all the way up to his neck. "That is the way for a glass vessel to travel," he said. And while some of the people he met felt sorry for him, or thought him strange, many of them appreciated his wise insights. He built quite a reputation for himself.

Things went on in this way for two years. Tomás toured the towns and villages of Spain, being introduced to people and asked to comment on the arts and fashions of the day. He even visited the royal court. But he always lived in fear, lest a trip or sudden collision cause his glass limbs to shatter.

One day, he met a Hieronymite monk who lived an austere life in the mountains, meditating and nursing the sick. With this quietly spiritual man, Tomás felt no need to come up with witty sayings. The two could simply talk as friends.

"What would you say," said the monk, "if I told you I am also made of glass?"

Tomás frowned. "But you're not."

"You don't believe me?" The monk raised an eyebrow.

"I didn't mean..." Tomás stuttered. He didn't want to offend the monk. But the man looked perfectly ordinary.

"Not on the outside," said the monk. "But I have a glass heart like yours."

Tomás looked at him. "Aren't you afraid it will shatter?"

"Not any more," said the monk. "Not since I joined the brotherhood. There are many hard things in this life, but some things are easier for the likes of me. Of *us*."

"You're…like me?" Tomás thought he was starting to understand.

"It's not something other people can see. And it's not always easy for them. But you don't have to be afraid. You won't shatter. You're stronger than that."

Tomás sat a little taller. "You're right," he said. And he undid the clasps of his iron bands. He took them off one by one and laid them on the ground. He unwound his cotton wadding, folded it up and placed it on the ground too. Then he shivered. He felt chilly in nothing but a long shirt and leggings.

"Would you like to try on some clothes?" said the monk. "We keep them for the poor."

"Yes, please," said Tomás. He chose a black doublet and breeches, and a pair of black boots.

"There. You look like a lawyer again," said the monk.

Tomás smiled. "How can I thank you?"

"Can I have a hug?" said the monk.

Tomás took a deep breath. "All right, then."

Cautiously at first, then a little more boldly, Tomás and the monk hugged. Nothing shattered. Nobody broke.

Tomás walked back down the mountain with a smile on his face, knowing he was not alone.

The Wife with the
Flying Head

10

The Wife with the Flying Head

I first came across this story in Jen Campbell's The Sister Who Ate Her Brothers *(2021). As soon as I read it, I knew I wanted to retell it. The symbolism really related to my experience of being a married ace. I traced a source tale in the* Journal of American Folklore *(1907). That version is taken from El Salvador, but there are versions of the 'flying head' myth across Southeast Asia and Latin America, including Malaysia, the Philippines, Cambodia, Thailand, Bali, Chile and Argentina. Readers from those cultures may recognise it as a vampiric creature, but my intention in this story is something quite different.*

There was once a wife and a husband who loved each other and wanted to have children. But when they went to bed, something strange happened. Every time they tried to make love, the wife's head detached from her body.

It wasn't particularly gory. The head simply popped off and then flew out of the window, with the wife's long black hair streaming behind it. It looked like a bizarre comet. The husband was left in bed with a headless body. And although it was the body of his beloved wife, it was something of a turn-off. The head never returned until morning, after the frustrated husband had finally fallen asleep.

"What's going on?" the husband said, after a fortnight of this odd behaviour. He felt he had been unusually patient in waiting that long. But it was such a very unexpected thing to have witnessed that he had to be sure it wasn't a dream.

The wife gave a happy sigh. "Oh, it's wonderful! I fly to all sorts of remarkable places. Up on the mountaintops with the eagles, down into the coral reefs, out into space among the stars. You should see it, husband."

"Never mind the stars!" the husband spluttered. "You...you should be here with me." He took a deep breath and tried again. "Don't you want to make love with me?"

"Well, I do love you," said the wife.

"And I love you," said the husband.

"And I'd like to have children."

"Well then, let's make love tonight," the husband said.

The wife agreed, and they tried again. But exactly the same thing happened. As soon as their lovemaking began, the wife's head popped off her body and flew out of the window.

"You did it again," said the husband the next morning.

"Yes, I can't seem to help it," the wife agreed.

"Are you sure you love me?" said the husband.

"Yes." The wife looked at her toes, then out at the tree in the garden. "I just can't seem to feel any..."

"What?" The husband gripped the sheet.

"Well, couldn't you just get on with it while I'm flying about? That would be a good solution."

The husband leapt out of bed. "I'm not doing it with a headless corpse! What do you take me for?"

"Sorry," said the wife. "That sounded better in my head. No pun intended."

The husband sighed. "Let's just try again."

But the same thing happened. This time, the husband stayed awake. He leaned out of the window. "Come back!" he shouted.

The wife's head came flying back. It attached itself to the husband's shoulder.

"What are you doing?" the husband cried. He tried to twist his own head round so that he could look his wife in the eyes. "That's not the part of your body you're supposed to join to mine."

"But this is where I love you," said the wife. "It's better in my head."

"Better for whom?" the husband muttered.

"I heard that," said the wife's head, and it flew off again.

*

84

The husband was angry now. He started to think his wife must be a witch, so he consulted a local priest.

"You must rub salt and ashes on the real body, so the witch cannot return to it," the priest instructed him. "Then you must make your wife a new body from the wood of a red mamey tree. The head will attach to that instead. The new wife will be much more obedient, I'm sure."

The husband did as the priest instructed. When the wife's head came back and saw the husband asleep and the outline of a body beside him, she assumed it was her real body. She attached to it and fell asleep.

When the husband woke in the morning, he expected to find a new and improved version of his wife. But on pulling back the covers, he found he was sleeping next to a tree! Growing from the top of it was a large, brown mamey apple with his wife's face.

The husband burst into tears. "I'm sorry, I'm sorry. Why did I ever listen to that wicked priest? You're not a witch," he sobbed. "You're my wife and I love you."

In sorrow, the husband planted the tree in the garden. He sat under it, winter and summer, talking to it. When the wind blew, he thought he could hear his wife singing.

One moonlit night near summer's end, the husband went out to the tree and saw something new. Hundreds of tiny fruits had grown on the branches. The fruits burst open, and out jumped hundreds of tiny children.

"Are you our father?" they cried. "Where is our mother?"

Tears came to the husband's eyes. He pointed to the tree. "There is your mother," he said. "But I don't know how she will feed you."

"Don't worry about that," said a voice from the sky. "I will feed them."

The husband looked up. It was the moon speaking. She sent bamboo sticks full of milk sliding down her moonbeams to feed the children. When they had drunk the milk, they became strong.

"Now we will restore our mother," they said.

They ran and fetched their mother's body, still preserved in salt and ashes. They picked the large mamey apple from the top of the tree and attached it to the body, pouring a little moon-milk over it. In the twinkling of an eye, the wife stood up, herself once more.

The husband knelt at her feet. "Can you forgive me?" he said.

The wife nodded. "I saw your tears. I heard your words to me as you sat under my branches all those months. You are forgiven." She spread her arms wide. "And look! We have more children than I could ever have hoped for."

From that time on, the husband and the wife brought up their children as good parents.

When they grew up, the tallest girl, who had her mother's black hair and was named Xochit Sihuat ('The Flower Girl'), said to her parents, "I'm going to stay a virgin all my life. I shall give my body to no one."

"Is that all right?" said the wife to her now-middle-aged husband. "You're not going to call her a witch?"

The husband laughed and shook his head. "Absolutely not. I learned my lesson long ago!"

Telling the Bees

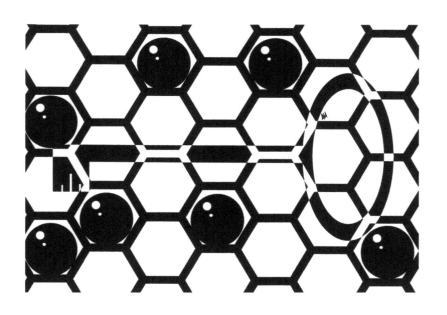

11

Telling the Bees

Bees are fascinating creatures with a lot of folklore attached to them. They once symbolised immortality, rebirth, purity and the soul. They were believed to be parthenogenic, and so signified virginity and chastity. In fact, the queen bee does mate (although the act of mating is death to the drones who mate with her). She then stores the sperm inside her and fertilises her own eggs with it – but only if the egg is to become a worker or a queen (i.e. a female). The drones (males) are born by parthenogenesis, from the unfertilised eggs. Bees were also once regarded as androgynous, which is one reason why I wanted to make the hero of this tale a non-binary character.

'Telling the Bees' is inspired by 'The Queen Bee' from the Brothers Grimm, and 'The Honey Mill' (2013), a reworking of that tale by Sylvia V Linsteadt, which first appeared in her Gray Fox Epistles. *It is named for the old European custom of 'telling the bees' about important events such as births, marriages, deaths and even Christmas. The name of Thalia is inspired by 'Sun, Moon and Talia', the 'Sleeping Beauty' tale from* The Tale of Tales.

This story is also a timely reminder of the importance of bees. We need them and they need us. Let's do all we can to preserve them.

A prince once had three children: Herman, Wendell and Golden. Herman was a mighty warrior and a hunter. Wendell was a shrewd and calculating tactician. But Golden was different. While Herman and Wendell had beards and hairy chests to be proud of, Golden looked neither male nor female. They felt that way too, much to their brothers' confusion. On top of that, Golden was a virgin, and showed no signs of wanting to stop being one.

This was too much for their brothers. What they couldn't understand, they mocked. "What's wrong with you, Golden?" they said. "You're not normal."

Golden didn't know the answers. But whenever they felt lonely, they went and talked to the bees on their father's estate. "There's nothing wrong with me," they said. "I'm just not like my brothers. And I would like to meet someone. I'm not sure what I'd like to happen, but I'd definitely like a soulmate."

The hum of the bees as they went in and out of their hives comforted Golden. "Soulmates are good," they seemed to say. "We in the hive think and feel as one. Some of us forage, some of us clean, some of us care for our growing children. Only the queen bee bears children, and the drones who mate with her die. But we are all soulmates. In summer we harvest, in winter we sleep and dream of the sun's light and warmth preserved in our sacred honey."

One summer, Herman and Wendell travelled far from home. When they didn't return, their father the prince became worried.

"I fear they have fallen into bad ways," he told the princess. "Started fights, or racked up gambling debts, or got some poor girls pregnant. Perhaps they're in prison."

"Don't fret," the princess said. "We'll send Golden to look for them."

"*Golden?*" The prince raised an eyebrow, but he didn't like to quarrel with his wife. So Golden was summoned and given their mission.

"I'm going on an adventure," they told the bees. "Wish me luck!"

As it happened, Herman and Wendell were not in prison, but lost in a forest, having argued about directions. And that was where Golden found them.

"I can't see that you'll be of any use," said Herman, when Golden arrived.

Golden just shrugged. "How about we go back the way I came?"

But it was an enchanted forest, and soon Golden was just as lost as the other two.

"We should have known better than to trust you," said Wendell. He rubbed his belly. "I'm starving!"

Golden stood still. They could hear a familiar humming. "Bees!"

They raced to follow the sound. Sure enough, there in a tree was a wild honeycomb. Teardrop-shaped waxen sheets hung from a branch with bees crawling over it and flying all around.

"I'll have some of that!" said Herman and Wendell together. They each began to shin up the tree and break off bits of honeycomb. The bees swarmed around them, humming at an anxious pitch and stinging the invaders. Herman and Wendell cursed and swatted them, leaping down and stamping them under their boots.

"Stop it!" Golden protested. "You're not doing it right. Bees die when they sting, you know."

"Shut up!" said Wendell, and crushed another bee.

Golden stood with their arms outstretched and started to hum. The bees drifted towards them like an amber cloud and covered their arms, legs, head and torso. Golden wasn't afraid. They closed their eyes and kept humming.

"Thank you," the bees hummed. "Not many humans would help us like that."

"Let's just say I know how it feels to be misunderstood," said Golden. "Besides, I suppose you're cousins of my bees at home."

The bees hummed together. "Ah, yes. You told your troubles to the bees. Let us repay your kindness and guide you in the right direction."

With that, they began to fly in a line, leading the way between the trees, uphill and down dale, with Golden following. Herman and Wendell brought up the rear, their faces sticky with honey.

They soon came to a clearing, in which stood the most marvellous palace. It looked remarkably similar to the siblings' palace at home, but it was made entirely of beeswax. Every turret and window ledge was formed from the tessellation of tiny wax hexagons, which gave off a scent of clover meadows. The palace was surrounded by a curtain wall – also of wax – through which the royal siblings entered and began to explore. They didn't see another living soul. Among the outbuildings was a stable, in which several stone horses stood in the stalls. One of them was covered in moss, and another's back was starting to crumble away. They were the only things in sight that weren't made of wax.

Going inside the palace, they found it similarly deserted. At last they came to a door with three locks. Each put an eye to the keyhole and looked. Inside the room was a tiny man with a long grey beard, sitting at a table.

Herman knocked. "Open up, Stump-Legs!"

Wendell knocked. "Hurry up, Badger-Beard!"

Finally, Golden knocked. "Good day to you, Grandfather. Can you let us in, please?"

The old man opened the door, but did not speak a word. He showed the three siblings to a table filled with food, and they ate their fill. Then he showed them to three beds, where they stretched out their limbs and dozed, tired from all their walking. At last he led them back to the table where they had found him sitting. It was piled high with wax tablets. He pointed to the topmost of them.

"Speak up! It's rude to point." Herman cuffed the old man on the back of his head.

"Are you stupid or what?" Wendell scoffed.

Golden stared fiercely at their brothers. "Just because he can't speak, that doesn't mean he's stupid. And so what if he was? He can still be good." They bowed to the man. "Thank you for your hospitality. Please help us to understand."

The man took Golden by the sleeve and led them through a passage-way, until a scent of honey and a sound of humming grew stronger. Suddenly, the passageway opened out into a large chamber with a vaulted ceiling. Inside was a giant comb of hexagonal chambers; more than Golden could count. Each one was sealed with transparent wax, and each contained a sleeping person. Tall and short, male and female, black and white, and every gradation in between.

Herman and Wendell stumbled in behind Golden, their mouths hanging open. It was hard to tell if the sleeping people were real or wax models.

"There are some real sleeping beauties here." Herman twirled his moustache.

Just a couple of these wax anatomical models could make me piles of gold, thought Wendell.

"I'll have some of that!" they both said.

The little grey-bearded man raised an eyebrow. He led the siblings back to the desk and pointed again at the topmost tablet. Golden leaned closer and read aloud:

Princess Thalia's Conditions for Finding a Soulmate

1. *Find the pearls. A thousand lie buried under the moss of the wood.*
2. *Find the key. Only one will unlock my sleeping chamber.*
3. *Find me. Only my soulmate will know me among the sleepers.*
4. *Fail before sunset and you will turn to stone.*

Herman rubbed his thighs. "Step aside, little siblings! I'm going to snare a princess!" He went into the forest and began digging under the moss with his nails. Sure enough, he soon felt smooth pearls under his fingertips. One here; another there. This is easy! he thought.

But it was not so easy as that. For every handful of pearls he piled up on the forest floor, another would vanish back underground as if they had never been unearthed. By the time the sun set, he had only just managed to retain a hundred. His limbs grew heavy. His movements slowed. By the time the others found him, he had turned to stone. It was too dark to do any more, so they slept in the wax palace that night.

In the morning, Wendell elbowed his way to the door. "I'll sort this out," he said.

But he fared no better than Herman. For every handful of pearls he gathered, another would vanish back underground. He tried digging little hollows to keep them in, and managed to retain nearly two hundred. But as the sun set, he felt his limbs grow heavy and his movements slow.

When Golden came to find him, Wendell too had turned to stone. "Oh, brothers!" Golden sighed. "If only you listened more than you spoke, and gave more than you took."

They went back into the palace – alone but for the silent little man – and lay on their bed. The buzz of bees thrummed in the waxen walls. Golden closed their eyes. The sound was familiar, comforting. It must be nice to sleep in a cocoon, they thought.

"Oh, it is," came the sound of many voices. "Some of us have slept here many years – others need only a short time cocooned from the world outside."

"You came here of your own accord?" Golden asked. But their lips never moved. They thought they might be dreaming.

"Yes, and for many reasons," came the reply. "Some wish to remain virgins, others wish to be virgins once more. Some are incapable of giving their bodies, others are incapable of giving their hearts. Some have been hurt, some are afraid, some just need time to get to know themselves."

"And what of Princess Thalia?" Golden asked. "What does *she* want?"

"A soulmate," said the voices. "Someone to share her secrets and dreams. Someone to whom she can open her heart. Someone to love and treasure."

"Someone to love and treasure," Golden repeated. They felt like they were falling into honey. "Someone to whom she can open her heart. I think I understand. The thousand pearls buried under the moss are the thousand sleepers. The key to open Thalia's cocoon is an understanding heart. And I'll know Thalia because..." Sleep covered them in a shimmering blanket.

When they awoke, Golden's bed was enclosed in fragrant beeswax. A peaceful humming filled the air. They sat up and broke off a piece of wax, then stood and looked around. The bed in which they had been sleeping was part of the comb in the vaulted chamber. A thousand souls slumbered in hexagonal bunks; bees went from mouth to mouth, feeding them honey. Golden looked at the fragment of wax in their hand. It looked just like a key.

They clambered up the bunks until they reached the very top one. Inside, a woman was sleeping, her hair and clothes covered in pearls. Golden put the key in the lock and turned it. Thalia sat up and smiled.

"Hello, Golden," she said. "I was dreaming about you."

"It's a shame about my brothers," said Golden. "Can nothing else be done for them?"

They, Thalia and the little grey-bearded man had just finished carrying Herman and Wendell's stony forms into the palace and laying each in a hexagonal bunk.

Thalia ran a hand through her hair. Golden thought she looked beautiful.

"It's the only way to get them to soften up. We'll come back and check on them after we've seen your parents." She smiled at Golden. "Maybe they'll get to know themselves better."

"I hope so," said Golden. They took Thalia's hand.

The Mirror

12

The Mirror

*The inclusion of the next three stories in this collection reflects a song I wrote
when I was still trying to figure out my identity:*

Who haven't kissed the printless snow,
Who cannot see; they'll never know
Why you are beautiful to me,
Just like the boy you'll never be.
My paper prince, my mirror friend,
If I should reach my journey's end,
You'd only slip away again.
But I need that pain.

'Cause I'm walking in the wrong land.
My generation doesn't understand.
They want to reach the high,
But I would die
If I could only touch your hand.
Tell me why we cannot be
With those we close our eyes to see?
Or would the bubble burst if we should touch?
I thought as much.

*This first tale, 'The Mirror', is my retelling of yet another chapter from
Phantastes (1858) by the amazing George MacDonald. ('The Asexual
Planet' in Asexual Myths and Tales, and to a lesser extent, 'Pygmailion and
Galatea' in Asexual Fairy Tales, are inspired by the same book.) There is
a similar tale by Lord Dunsany, 'The Wonderful Window' (1912), which*

I have also made use of. I have given my story a slightly happier ending than either Dunsany's or MacDonald's because – much as I love a tragic romance – there can be such a thing as too much, and I didn't want my readers to feel that they were getting an ace version of the 'kill your gays' trope. There are times when things do feel hopeless, and you have to express that. But there are also times when you need to give hope to other people.

The mirror stood against the back wall of the antique shop. It was covered with dust, and far too tall for Cosmo's attic lodging room. But the symbols carved into its heavy wooden frame made Cosmo think of magic and long-forgotten kingdoms where faerie knights guarded castles washed by bubbling sea foam. "How much?" he asked the old shopkeeper.

The man named the price. At least, Cosmo thought at first that it was a man. But on second glance, it might just as easily have been a woman.

"I cannot afford that," he sighed.

"What *can* you afford?" said the shopkeeper.

Cosmo named a price that, in truth, was slightly higher than he could comfortably afford, but which he thought the shopkeeper would accept.

"In that case, that is the price of the mirror." The shopkeeper paused. "But if ever you wish to be rid of it, you must promise to return it to me."

"I promise," said Cosmo, though he had no intention of returning his prize. Paying the promised amount, he carried the mirror from the shop.

"Sold for the sixth time," the shopkeeper muttered, as the door fell shut with the clang of a little brass bell. "Let's see if this owner fares any better than the rest."

Cosmo carried the mirror to his lodgings: a long, low room at the top of one of the highest houses in town. It was rented, of course, for he was a student at the University of Prague and, though he was of noble birth, far from wealthy. The room was furnished with little more than an oaken clothes press, a faded couch and a couple of wooden chairs. But what it lacked in furniture, it made up for in oddities. For Cosmo's tastes lay in the macabre and the bizarre. His room boasted a full human skeleton suspended by a string, an antique sword and battle axe, a porcupine skin, and many strange herbs and powders. Yes, Cosmo was secretly a student of magic – but the theory of magic only. He had never been so presumptuous as to try casting a spell.

The next day, after lectures, Cosmo set about cleaning and examining his new treasure. He was sure he could make something of those symbols if he really tried. It is strange, though, he thought, how magical a mirror is in itself. My room reflected in the mirror looks like a room from a fairy tale. I'm sure that, if I could only get into that room and open the door I see, I would discover halls of marble statues that come to life and dance; forests so thick with butterflies that their wings would bear me up into the air.

As he thought this, he saw the door of the reflected room open. A woman clothed in white came gliding in, and lay down upon the couch. Cosmo's heart stuttered. How could that be? He turned to glance behind him at the couch in his real room, but there was no one there. Again he looked into the mirror. There was the woman! She did not appear to see him. In fact, she seemed unaware of her surroundings. She stretched herself out with a sigh and closed her eyes. Her chest heaved, and two large tears welled from beneath her closed eyelids. Cosmo hardly dared to breathe in case the vision vanished. He feared the woman's eyes would open and meet his.

For a long time, nothing happened. At last, the woman opened her eyes and looked around. Her glance fell on the skeleton, and she shuddered. Cosmo instantly felt ashamed of the thing. He would have removed it; only he feared to move in case the woman saw him. However, her eyes closed once more, her breathing fell into an even rhythm, and she slept. How long Cosmo watched her, he could not say. He was entranced. She was by far the most beautiful and magical person he had ever seen. At length, he picked up a book, and casually turned the pages. When he looked again, the woman was gone.

The scene in the mirror was robbed of its magic. It was merely a reflection of Cosmo's attic room: a dingy student lodging. The offending skeleton leered at him. Despite the late hour, he set about tidying it away, along with the other macabre objects, to a recess where they could cast no reflection in the mirror. It seemed like sacrilege to sleep on the couch where *she* had lain. But as he had no other bed, Cosmo was forced to do just that.

The next evening, he waited eagerly by the mirror. As the bells chimed six, the woman came gliding in once more, her white dress floating behind her. Though she still looked pained, Cosmo thought her less sad. Her eyes went to where the skeleton had been, and she gave a nod of satisfaction on finding it removed. This time, she seemed to pay more attention to her surroundings. But as before, she soon fell asleep upon the couch. Cosmo watched carefully. After some time, she rose languidly from the couch and drifted out like a sleepwalker.

A golden glow settled upon Cosmo's life. He had found magic! Gradually, he began to renovate his home for the benefit of his mysterious visitor. He gave fencing lessons to rich students and the young nobility of Prague. With the money he earned from this, he bought new furniture. Closets to house his strange apparatus. A new bed for himself, and a sumptuous couch for the lady. Curtains to screen his sleeping area from the lady's view. Each day, he added something new, and each night, the woman gave a look of acknowledgement, by which Cosmo guessed that his efforts pleased her. Yet still she looked pained, and still she wept and sighed. As for Cosmo, he had pains of his own. For he had fallen in love with the woman in the mirror. He knew it was but a shadow that he loved, but it seemed to him a higher love than any he had known in the world.

One night, the woman entered the mirror-room in a gown the colour of midnight, with diamonds at her throat. As she reclined on the couch, Cosmo felt such a pang of love that he was sure the lady must feel it too. And sure enough, a blush crept up her throat and brought fire to her cheeks, as if she read his thoughts. But presently another explanation came to Cosmo's mind. She has a lover somewhere, and she is thinking of him. All Cosmo's thoughts turned to jealousy at the thought of this unseen lover. For of course, she has a life in her own world. How could I ever think her mine?

Strange to say, the woman left the mirror earlier than usual that night. And the next night, she did not appear at all.

*

Now Cosmo was in torment. Where was she? And with whom? What was really behind that other door? Cosmo forgot to eat. He missed his lectures. He barely slept. For six nights, he waited by the mirror, gnawing at his nails and clawing his unshaven chin.

On the seventh night, he decided he could wait no more. Though he had studied magic in theory only, he determined to cast a spell. He took out his books of magic. For the next three nights, he read and made notes from midnight until three in the morning. He haunted odd parts of the city and acquired arcane ingredients. Those who passed him on the street shrank from his ghoulish features. But at last the spell was ready. Cosmo chalked the mystical symbols on the floorboards and began the incantation.

As the bells chimed six, reluctant, slow and stately, the lady glided in. As her face came into view, Cosmo caught his breath. She was wan and sickly with shadowed eyes, her jaw tense with pain. But Cosmo would not be deterred. With a deplorable word, he touched a taper to the brazier. It was a sultry evening, heavy with thunder. The purple air closed in around him, stealing his breath. The charcoal glowed first blue, then green. It cast a ghastly tinge over the woman's face. Her eyes widened. She saw Cosmo. He felt her soul beat against the glass like a moth. There was a desperate entreaty in her gaze...

The next moment, the door of Cosmo's room opened and the woman walked in. She was taller than he'd expected; imposing against the thundery twilight and the glow of a magic fire. Every inch of her was dripping wet. "Why did you summon me?" she said. "Why bring me here in the midst of a thunderstorm, through rain-soaked streets?"

"Because I am dying for love of you," Cosmo said. "I saw you in the mirror, and I cast the spell."

"*You* are dying?" The lady's voice rose. "I am the one doomed to lie in motionless trances day and night. I am the one whose soul is bound to the mirror. Voyeur after voyeur has watched me. I can do nothing to stop them. Six times now, the mirror has changed hands. And not one has dared to free me."

"Are you not free now?" Cosmo asked.

The lady scoffed. "I am in your power. But think not that your spell summoned me here. It was the strength of your desire. It draws my soul towards you, as the moon pulls the tides."

Cosmo blushed. "Can you love me, then?" He hardly dared hope.

The lady sighed. "I do not know. There are too many enchantments laid on me. Part of me feels that it would be a joy to lay my head on your bosom and weep to death. But I do not know if I can... I do not know."

"Please." Cosmo seized her hand.

The lady snatched it away. Her gaze became steely. "If you love me, set me free. Even from yourself. Break the mirror."

Cosmo swallowed. She was asking the impossible. "But would I ever see you again?"

"That is immaterial," said the lady.

A fierce war raged in Cosmo's breast. Break the mirror and he would lose all chance of summoning her again. But she had asked him to prove his love...

"Oh, he doesn't love me," the lady scoffed. "He is no better than the rest."

At this, Cosmo was seized with rage. He took up his antique sword by the scabbard and struck at the mirror with all the might he possessed. But the sword slipped from the scabbard and its pommel struck the wall instead. There was a deafening peal of thunder. Cosmo fell to the floor and hit his head. When he came to, both the lady and the mirror were gone.

For weeks afterwards, Cosmo lay in a fever, thrashing in damp sheets. When he came to himself, he was thin and feeble. He dragged himself from his bed and staggered back to the antique shop. "Where is the mirror?" he demanded. "The antique mirror I bought. Have you seen it?"

But the shopkeeper no longer seemed friendly. They grimaced at Cosmo with an evil laugh. "Spoiled your one chance, did you? You won't get the mirror back now."

Cosmo felt like throttling the old sinner, but he could get nothing more out of them. Magic! The whole thing reeked of enchantments. He no longer cared if he would see the lady again. He had failed her. In his heart, he asked whether the sword had truly slipped, or if he had been unable to do the deed. And now, another might have the mirror in their possession; one who might behave worse towards the lady than he had done. He now had but one mission: to find the mirror and break it.

He neglected his studies, his fencing lessons, his health. He went about with a silver hammer in his hand, listening to every snippet of gossip in every wine shop and beer hall, searching for the mirror's new owner.

"Have you seen Steinwald lately?" a fellow student asked him one day.

"No. He used to come to me for rapier lessons, but I supposed he didn't need them any more."

"It's odd," said the student. "No one has seen him since he visited that antique shop. Do you remember the one?"

That was all the hint Cosmo needed. Von Steinwald was a courtier, well known for his reckless habits and fierce passions. The idea that the lady of the mirror should fall into such hands...

Cosmo haunted Steinwald's house, until one night he saw it lit up, with music drifting from the windows and carriages pulling up outside. A party. Though he was now as gaunt as the skeleton that had so repelled the lady, Cosmo went home, brushed off his dress suit and chalked his kid gloves. He approached the house and swaggered up the front steps as though he were the kaiser himself, the silver hammer in his pocket...

In a lofty, silent chamber, a lady lay on her couch, so pale and still that she could have been a marble statue.

"It can't be long now," her women whispered. "She's barely woken for days."

Suddenly, the lady sat bolt upright and gasped. "Cosmo! He did it. I'm free!"

"My Lady..." A waiting-maid hurried to take her pulse.

"There's no time." The lady stood up. "Fetch my cloak, Lisa. I must go to him. Run!"

They ran like the wind towards one of the bridges over the Moldau. The moon was at its height and the streets were almost deserted. When the lady reached the bridge, she saw Cosmo leaning on the balustrade in his dress coat, his face white and trembling.

"Are you free, My Lady? Have I atoned for my error? Do I love you – truly?"

"Cosmo!" She ran to embrace him. "I know now that you love me. I am free of the mirror forever." But when she drew back, there was blood on her clothes, and on his hand where he had clutched at his side.

"Good... I am glad," he sighed, and sank to the ground.

When the maid arrived, the lady was holding a corpse.

The mirror hung on the wall of a chamber in the Schloss Hohenweiss. It was only a fragment, a shard pulled from the side of a dying man, but the Princess Von Hohenweiss was insistent. It must not be removed. If she peered closely into it, the fragment of her chamber that it reflected looked like a room from a fairy tale. One could imagine flying carpets coming in at the window.

Every evening, as the bells struck six, the princess positioned her chair before the shard of mirror. And in the tiny reflection, a man in evening dress with a silver hammer in his hand walked into the room, looked around with a smile, and lay down on the couch.

Paper Prince

13

Paper Prince

*By contrast with the previous tale, this one is unashamedly tragic. And
– pardon the pun – it is a mirror image of it.*

*Many of us have fallen in love with a fictional character. For some, they
will be the only love we ever have, or ever want to have. But what if a fantasy
character fell in love with one of us? What if the poster on the wall were
looking back? That would be a truly unrequited love story.*

In my homeland, invisibility is regarded as a gift. The fortunate
traveller who comes across the magic cloak, ring or potion that
can render him invisible has found a weapon with which to outwit
dragons, goblin hordes or evil sorcerers. For all my own gifts, I envy him,
whoever he may be.

But when she tells me that she is invisible outside this room, there
are tears in her eyes. No one sees her, she says. No one talks to her. It's
like they are walking straight through her. She might as well not be here,
she says. She might as well be dead. She cries when she says this, and I
long to comfort her, but drawing pins and the lack of a third dimension
restrain me.

She talks to me, she says, because there is no one else to talk to.
There are other people, though. I hear their voices calling to one another
and their footsteps running up and down the corridor. Perhaps they are
invisible too. I do not know. She talks to me about her lectures and
the changing weather outside. She reads to me too - stories from *The
Forgotten and the Fantastical*, interspersed with selections from Chaucer
and Malory, although she struggles a little with the accent. She wants to
be a librarian, or maybe something in a publishing house. She once had

ambitions to be a writer but gave up because she wasn't good enough. Her poetry is in a drawer with her reproduction elven jewellery. She doesn't read me that.

Not that it's all talk, you understand. Most of the time, when she comes in, she makes notes or writes essays with the music turned up. And at the weekend, she goes home. Then the room is dark and silent, and I am left to listen for the muffled shouts and laughter from happier places. Once, one of the invisible people in the corridor knocked on the door, but I couldn't go to answer it, being constantly frozen in a heroic pose, my sword unsheathed to protect absent friends. When she comes back, she is always happier. Her voice sounds calmer when she talks to me. She pecks me on the cheek and promises that this week will be better. Then she puts on her pyjamas and snuggles up in the duvet with her books. I try not to watch too much.

One night, there is a knock when she is around to answer it. I cannot see the door from my position, but I hear the voice.

"We're all going out for a drink. We just wondered if you wanted to come."

"Well...er..." Her voice has gone tense and squeaky. "No thanks. I've got a lot of work to do tonight."

She sits back down at the desk and carries on writing, but after ten minutes she stops and her head goes down to the book. I can hear her sobbing.

"I hate being me! Why am I so useless? Why am I so stupid as to think that I will be any different in a different place?"

The books fall on the floor. A page is bent, but she does not see. She leaves them. She kneels on the bed and spreads herself out across me, stroking my hair and kissing my lips. I am her prince, she says. No one understands her but me. She presses her cheek against mine and I almost believe I can feel her warm tears running down my face.

When it comes to exam time, she is quiet and determined. Some people are terrified of exams, she says. She isn't. If you know your subject, there is nothing to be afraid of. I am proud of her. I sense the determination in her kisses as she leaves for her unseen destination. She will start some new classes after the exams, she tells me. She will miss the old ones, but mostly she is looking forward to it. It has been hard, but she is trying to say hello to people she knows now. She still cries sometimes. My face gives her courage and my cloak absorbs her tears.

She gets good results. She pins them on the wall next to me when she comes in from her new class. She seems happier; she is singing under her breath. It is going to be fun, she says. This class is friendlier than the last one. They have discussions. The tutor makes them get into groups. Someone spoke to her in the library. She tells me this as though it were the greatest miracle on earth. It brings a smile to her face. She has a lovely smile; she does not smile enough, I think.

One afternoon I hear her voice in the corridor. She is speaking, not to me, but to those I cannot see. Voices reply to her. She sounds animated. When she comes back, I want to ask if she has lost her invisibility. Can they see her now? Can she see them? I do not know because, beyond this room, I see neither.

Another time she comes in and, instead of turning on the radio, goes straight to her bookcase. Then she turns to me and laughs. I won't believe this, she says, but in this morning's tutorial there was a discussion and she ended up paired with the same boy again – she's probably mentioned him before. It turns out he shares her taste in fiction. At home, he has a first edition of *The Hobbit* that was in his uncle's second-hand shop. They have just spent ages talking in the snack bar and nearly missed their lecture. She is going to lend him her copy of *The King of Elfland's Daughter*. She kisses the tip of her finger and touches my cheek with it, before whirling back to the bookcase. The spell is broken; I am happy for her. But I know that she has not mentioned this boy to me before. Perhaps she has forgotten. Her back is to me. A pretty spring skirt swings gently from her slender hips. Her hair is long with tiny braids in it. She finds the book and drifts from the room like the dryads in the forests at home.

She sings a lot now. The strain of music follows her in and out of the room. There is a new light in her eyes. She smiles to herself. She stands in front of the mirror, arranging her hair and her jewellery. "How do I look?" she asks me; then she blushes and laughs because she no longer expects me to answer. And, if I could, I do not think I could find the words.

She is not in the room as much as she used to be. The cosy winter evenings wrapped in the duvet have given way to light, warm nights when she flies to the corridor on even lighter feet. The well-thumbed anthologies lie untouched on the shelf. I miss their familiar stories and the voice that told them. She speaks to me less and less. She does not notice it; she does not mean to do it. The sobbing face that pressed itself against my nerveless cheek is gone. Sometimes she winks at me as she comes in or goes out. And then the click of the closing door brings a silence sadder than a room full of tears.

She is not going home this weekend. I expected her travel bag to be on the bed by lunchtime, but it never appeared. Instead the door opens and I see her coming into the room. A shy smile lights up her features, but she is not looking at me. She is not alone. A boy comes in behind her. He is lanky and young. They are talking and laughing together. He looks at her the way I would if my expression could change. I would tighten my grip on my sword hilt, but my hand can never move. She is making drinks, opening and shutting drawers. He is leafing through her books. I feel like a voyeur. I want to leave but I am pinned to the wall and – now I see – I am no longer any better than wallpaper. They are sitting on the bed with their backs against me. I can see the words of the poetry in her hand.

"No, you must read it to me," the young man says. "I'm sure it's very good."

She settles down to read and, as she begins, I would gladly take any gift rather than this one, goblin hordes or no. I am invisible. I might as well not be here. There is no one I can talk to; no one sees my pain. My heart is breaking, but I will never be able to shed a single tear.

Bursting the Bubble

14

Bursting the Bubble

This is a wholly original fantasy story that first appeared in Vitality *magazine in December 2015. It is inspired by the surreal painting* Twist of Local Geography *by Russian-born artist Michael Cheval.*

It was liberating to be able to create the character of Lyra as a middle-aged asexual woman who has been married and has a son. As it's historical fantasy, I didn't want to define Silverlace and Mallow by modern terms. They are who they are.

"Come and see, Mallow."

I seized his hand and dragged him through the Geometric Courtyard. His high-pitched laughter echoed from the quadrangle walls as I guided him between herbal flower beds in the shape of alchemical symbols.

"Slow down, Lyra. I'm going to trip. I'm not getting any younger, you know."

I paused at the foot of the spiral staircase and let him catch his breath. He was still as cherub-faced as he had been at nineteen, but in recent months his moss-green livery had become tighter around the waist. Unwanted weight gain: the eunuch's eternal curse.

"You can't be old," I said. "You're six months younger than me, and I'm young."

"Anything you say." He grinned. Then he nodded up to the triple-arched window above us. "Are you sure this is a good idea? Silverlace may not like my intruding."

"It's fine." I took his hand again and started up the staircase. "Silverlace is so proud of this one, he won't care if I invite the whole court."

All the same, at the top of the stairs I paused to put my dress and wimple in order. I was the first all-female assistant Silverlace had ever taken, and I had no intention of losing his good opinion.

"Is that you, Lyra?" Silverlace's voice always reminded me of a jackdaw's caw.

"Yes. I've brought Mallow to see how the bubbles are coming on."

I tiptoed into the laboratory, pulling Mallow after me. He took his hand from mine and made the customary two-thirds bow to Silverlace. The royal alchemist outranked a court eunuch, but only by so much. We hadn't yet worked out where an alchemist's assistant ranked, when that assistant was also a guardsman's widow and the mother of a guardsman. A generic curtsy usually did the job well enough.

Silverlace was standing by the pedestal that supported the parent bubble, a book of formulae in his hand. Everyone at court said 'he' and 'his', although these were woefully inadequate words for the person Silverlace was. Right now he looked male, his blue frock coat open to display his lace cravat; the starry diadem of his office sitting regally on his brow. But that look could change in a moment. Behind the mask of white face paint, the features outlined with black, lay depths the queen herself couldn't fathom.

"They are still in prototype but the tests are proceeding well." Silverlace gestured vaguely towards the pedestal. "When they are complete, the queen should be able to view all parts of the realm in detail – a skill her forebears could only dream of."

Impatience got the better of me. "Look, Mallow. You see this big bubble? You can see the whole realm in it." I led him towards the pedestal, where the entire country was spread out like a toy town, contained within a giant bubble. Rivers like silver threads flowed into the sea; tiny waterfalls foamed; herds of deer migrated, each animal the size of a dust mote.

"Remarkable!" Mallow breathed.

"Oh, but that's not the best bit." Inside, I wanted to dance with excitement like a child. "They give birth." Gently, I lifted a smaller bubble from a pedestal half the size of the first. "This is one we birthed from Kenbright Province. Look!"

I held it up so he could see the province filling the smaller bubble. Mallow's breath was coming faster.

"More detail, see?" I pointed. "Look, there's a little town. You can see the market."

"And how close up do they go?" Mallow's eye went to the collection of bubbles of varying sizes occupying shelves, bowls, even windowsills.

"This is the smallest one we've birthed so far." I picked up a bubble the size of a peach. "The whole thing is just one village. Somewhere in the Borderlands, I think... Mallow, what's wrong?"

Mallow's face suddenly looked very strange. His mouth was opening and shutting. His cheeks were flushed. "That's my... That's my village." His voice cracked. "That's where I was born."

"Really?" I leaned over, interested. I knew next to nothing about Mallow's past.

Then a cry made me leap backwards. I looked at Mallow. He had tears in his eyes.

"Gods be merciful!" he said. "That's my sister."

I had come to an understanding of myself later in life than most. Silverlace, I suspected, had become aware of his dual soul as soon as he was old enough to notice his dual body. I had merely assumed that I was a good virgin and that desire would come once I was married. It didn't. I respected and cared for my husband, and was thrilled to give birth to his child, but we never had another. After years of physicians and counsellors, he came to realise that this was simply who I was. When he fell in battle, I mourned him. By then, our son Cob was already set to follow in his father's footsteps. I knew that a second marriage would be a lie. Never again would I make vows that I had no intention of keeping. But I needed a soulmate, someone to love. Someone who had no designs on my body. So I loved Mallow. I loved him with all my heart, and I could not bear the thought of ever losing him.

The day after I had shown Mallow the bubbles, I came to the laboratory to find him there alone. He was sitting at my workbench with the smallest bubble in his hand, staring, staring. He never even saw me until I put a hand on his shoulder, and then he jumped as if a musket had gone off.

"Forgive me." His dreamy eyes came back into focus. "Silverlace said I could look if I left a record of my observations." He gestured towards a logbook.

I was about to reply, but his attention was drawn back to the bubble. "She's pegging out the washing." He spoke as if this were an unheard-of achievement. "An hour ago she put out some crumbs for the birds."

He'd been here an hour? I tried to swallow the uncomfortable feeling in my chest. "I didn't know you had a sister."

"Twin sister. Columbine." He gave a sigh. "Gods, but we were so close! Like two halves of a walnut. I never realised until now just how much I miss her."

I reached out to touch his shoulder again, but drew back at the last moment and left him to his staring.

He found a way to visit the laboratory every day. Silverlace and I were working on second and third versions of the original prototypes. The queen had asked to see our work by May Fest and nothing could be allowed to go wrong. Mallow's bubble (as I couldn't help thinking of it) remained the smallest and most detailed we had managed to produce. Thanks to his constant note-taking, it was also the one we had the most data on.

"It is the chief exhibit," Silverlace insisted, one time when I suggested Mallow let the bubble alone and go about his own duties again. "To achieve this level of detail is a true breakthrough in alchemy. The queen will throw open the coffers when she sees what we have done here." He gave a maternal smile, the black diamonds on his cheeks creasing. "Besides, I thought you would enjoy having your...ah...playmate work alongside us for a time."

Playmate! I stabbed the nib of my quill right through the parchment. Silverlace's banter would be easier to take had Mallow paid me the least attention lately. But all he seemed to care for nowadays was the minuscule figure in the bubble.

"She has been to the butcher's and bought a fine capon," was all his talk one day. The next, "It has rained all day. Her poor flower beds are quite flattened." Another day, he was all anxiety. "I haven't seen her once today. Do you think she is unwell?"

"Perhaps she's sick of you looking at her," I said. It came out rather more harshly than I intended.

Mallow looked up; his eyes wide beneath his yellow cowl. "Lyra!

I never expected to hear such words from you. You of all people should know how it feels to miss a loved one."

"Indeed I do!" I waited for him to realise what I was getting at. Instead, he went back to staring at his wretched bubble.

I started to dream of pins.

Each year on the eve of May Fest, the queen held a court masque in the Chessboard Garden. Favoured courtiers were selected to dress as the pieces and enact a performance that was half game, half ballet. First fruits were sampled. Wine flowed. And from least to greatest, the whole court was invited. I had spent weeks working on my dress. It was only my second May Fest as assistant alchemist, and I wanted to achieve a look that conveyed my status while still remaining pretty and springlike. To that end, I had replaced the usual plain gold epaulettes on my gown with chiffon ones embroidered with cherry blossom. The same pattern decorated the border of my wimple. I had spent hours sewing by candlelight, long after my work with Silverlace was over. With every stitch, I had imagined the look on Mallow's face when he saw my handiwork.

By twilight, the specially erected scaffolding around the chessboard was already half full, excited revellers laughing and chatting as footmen went about lighting the flambeaux. I waited for Mallow beneath our usual pear tree until three sides of the chessboard were illuminated and the footmen were beginning on the fourth. Then I picked up my skirts and ran for the laboratory, anger building as I grew hotter and hotter.

I flung the door open so that it crashed against the wall. He didn't even look up. My jaw clenched as I realised that he hadn't even changed out of his everyday livery. An insipid smile played over his lips as he stared into the bubble.

"Mallow!"

It was impossible that he could fail to hear. My bellow seared my throat. Magpies took off from the windowsill with a "Crarc-crarc-crarc" and a great flapping of wings. Glass bottles chinked together on shelves. Mallow leapt to his feet, his eyes saucer-wide. Instinctively, his fingers gripped the bubble tighter, pointed nails digging in hard. Too hard. There was a roar like cannon fire, and Mallow fell back with a cry. The space where – a moment before – a bubble had contained a whole village was filled with brown smoke and an acrid smell.

"Lyra! What in the name of seven hells is going on here?"

In the moment it took for me to register the presence of Silverlace, resplendent in his dress robes and make-up, framed in the doorway, his expression one of fury. But it wasn't the torrent of curses that spewed from his mouth, nor the certain knowledge that I would be out of work tomorrow, that hurt me most. It was the look of utter devastation on Mallow's face.

I sat in the window seat of my apartment, tracing the braid on my late husband's guardsman's jacket. It was the only thing of his that I had kept. If I held it very close, I could still discern a hint of his scent; the scent of a simple man, a soldier, much like our son, who had hoped his wife would share with him an understanding born of mutual desire. I had failed him, as I had failed Silverlace by my unprofessional conduct. As I had failed Mallow with my jealousy. He had only wanted to see his sister; what was wrong with that? Had one of those bubbles unexpectedly revealed Cob on his tour of duty, would I have acted any differently? How ridiculous to expect a friend, a lover – whatever you choose to name your closest companions – to have eyes only for you and your view of the world. What person on earth lived like that?

Silverlace would be in the throne room now, trying to salvage his project from the wreckage I had made of it. Attempting his grand presentation without its glorious centrepiece. Would he even let me know the outcome? Or would I have to wait, like so many, for the slow progress of the court gossip train; the chambers of military widows being the last place its wagons stopped?

I thought again of Mallow and sighed. How he must hate me now! He had found his first link to family in years and I had stolen it from him. My throat tightened and I hugged the jacket closer. Family. Mine was far from me now. I had hoped that Mallow and I were a new sort of family; a family of choice. Yes, and Silverlace too, for all his cawing. Tears spilled from my eyes and I started to sob. I had lost everything. All I had for comfort was the empty jacket of a long-dead man who had never understood me anyway.

"Lyra?"

For a moment, the light voice made me think that Cob had come running in from the schoolroom with a cut knee, until I remembered that Cob was now a guardsman with a full beard, and only ever called me Mother anyway. The person standing in the doorway would never have a beard, nor a man's voice, however old he grew. But he was not old. I had told him that before.

"Mallow, I…" Shame burnt my cheeks and made my tears flow faster. "What I did to you was unforgivable. I'm so sorry."

"I went to the queen." Mallow's words came out in a rush. "I begged her to reinstate you. Told her it wasn't your fault. That Silverlace must have overreacted."

The enormity of his words stopped my tears with a jolt. "You did what? Mallow, you know the penalties for approaching the queen unscheduled. You could have been banished. Why?"

"Why do you think?" He looked me in the eye for the first time since this conversation had begun. "Lyra, have you been crying? Come here, you silly fool. It's all right."

I buried my face in the softness of his tunic. His hug was warm and comforting. I had no idea how much I'd missed it. "I thought you'd be angry with me," I said into his shoulder.

"I was," he said, "for a while. But then I thought about it from your point of view. I must have really hurt you, Lyra. I'm sorry."

"No, I'm sorry." I stepped back and straightened my wimple. "We'll birth a new bubble. We'll find your sister again."

"She won't take your place." Mallow suddenly looked about fifteen, cherub features and all. "What we have is special."

"Special," I agreed. I let out a deep breath, exhaling my troubles with it. "So. The May Dance. Got a partner yet?"

"Aren't we a bit old for that?"

I raised my eyebrows in mock scandal. "You're not old until I am. And I'm definitely young."

"So you are, Madam Assistant Alchemist." He offered me his arm. "To the maypole, then."

Eyes Made of Salt

15

Eyes Made of Salt

It's no secret that I love 'women in towers' stories. But 'men in towers' stories are harder to come by. This is my attempt to draw together two such stories: one from my native West Yorkshire, and one from the Hindu epic, the Mahabharata. Since the latter is a religious text, I didn't want to mess about with it. So I created a framing story to draw the two together, partly inspired by a prompt from the Magic Realism Bot on Twitter.

The Woman has walked many miles to find the inn. It stands in the crevice of a mountain pass. The inn provides food and shelter to pilgrims and traders crossing the mountains, and has saved many lives. But the Woman is no pilgrim. Nor is she a trader. She is not content to sit by the hearth in the downstairs snug, eating a bowl of stew. Nor will she retire to a bunk in one of the ground-floor dormitories, weary though she is.

She climbs the winding staircase of the tower at the inn's centre. On its topmost point is a lamp, guiding travellers to safety. Below the eaves of the roof nest the ravens, whose black wings carry messages far and near. But the Woman need not climb so high. She seeks out the Innkeeper, whose rooms stand at an imposing height. He has never left the tower in all the years the inn has stood. But the Woman has been sent by Fate herself. She cannot be refused.

The Innkeeper's eyes are an opaque white. But he knows she is there. "It was only a matter of time," he says. "And now you will try to persuade me?"

"That's not how it works," says the Woman. "Let me tell you a story."

*

There was once a rich man in the West Riding of Yorkshire who fell foul of a witch. He passed her on horseback when her child had fallen into a ditch, and refused to dismount and help her. For this, the witch cursed him. "You will have a son who will die on his twenty-first birthday."

The man feared a witch's curse. So, when his son was born, he had a tower built on the moors, with no door and only one high window, too far above ground to serve as an exit. There the son lived with just a manservant for company. Their daily supplies were sent up by ropes in a basket, and their waste was removed the same way. Thus they lived for many years.

On the day the boy turned twenty-one, the weather was bitterly cold. The son and his keeper called out for more firewood to keep the tower warm. The wood was sent up in a basket, as usual. But when the lad threw the sticks on the fire, a snake came slithering out and bit him. He died from the poison that very day.

So the witch's prophecy was fulfilled.

"You're talking to the wrong man," says the Innkeeper. "My snake is harmless. It is not my fate to be bitten."

"Then let me tell you another story," the Woman says.

The Hindu sacred scriptures tell of a sage named Rishyasringa. He was born, miraculously, of a hind. This hind had come to drink the waters of the lake, and in so doing drank the seed of the rishi Vibhandaka, who lived a hermit's life in the forest. His seed had gone into the water as he washed. For this reason, Rishyasringa was born with the antlers of a deer and the purity of a saint. His father raised him secretly in the forest, so he never saw another human soul, nor knew what a woman was.

But King Romapada of Anga had been given a prophecy that drought would end and fertility return to his land with the coming of Rishyasringa. He summoned his royal courtesans to entice Rishyasringa from his home. But the courtesans were too afraid of the consequences should they seduce a sage.

Then an old courtesan spoke up. "Your Majesty, give me a ship decorated with plants and flowers, and loaded with all kinds of fruit, sweetmeats and wine. Give me a selection of your most beautiful courtesans, and set the ship to float downriver into the depths of the forest. I will bring you Rishyasringa."

Rishyasringa was alone in his hermitage when the boat arrived. His father Vibhandaka had gone to town to buy supplies. The old courtesan sent her daughter to seek out Rishyasringa. When he saw her, he was overcome. He had never seen such a beautiful human being before.

"Are you a god?" he breathed. "How may I worship you?"

The courtesan's daughter laughed. "Oh no, my young rishi! You have got it wrong. It is I who must worship you. That is my religion."

She sat by Rishyasringa's side and put her arm about him. He felt shivers run over his body. She fed him wine and sweetmeats. She kissed and caressed him. Rishyasringa was in a trance. By the time she left, all he wanted was to see her again.

When Vibhandaka returned home, he looked at his son in horror. "Are you drunk? What has become of you?"

"Oh, Father," Rishyasringa sighed. "A young rishi came to visit me today. I think he was a god in disguise. He had long hair, and his body was soft. His clothes were smooth, not roughly spun like ours. He fed me strange, sweet fruit that had no skin or seeds, and a drink that made me happy. He was beautiful, Father! I want to be with him."

When Vibhandaka heard this, he knew that a woman had been with his son. "That was no god!" he said. "That was a demon. They come in beautiful disguises to tempt us from our religious duty. See how it has tempted you to drink wine, and now you are drunk! If that demon comes again, you resist it and send it away!" Then he went out and searched the forest for the woman, but she was nowhere to be found.

However, the next time Vibhandaka was away from home, the courtesan's daughter visited once more. This time, Rishyasringa was waiting for her.

"Take me to your hermitage. Please," he begged. "Before my father comes back."

The courtesan's daughter smiled to herself. "Certainly." She took Rishyasringa to the boat, which was all covered with plants. "Here is my hermitage," she said. "Step inside."

Together with the girl, Rishyasringa stepped into the boat and began to take his pleasure as it sailed away. A floating hermitage, he thought, through the cloud of intoxication. How novel!

When the boat reached the kingdom of Anga, they found a hermitage on the banks of the river. Upon the old courtesan's instructions, the king had given orders for it to be built there.

"Come," said the courtesan's daughter to Rishyasringa. "Here is my permanent place of prayer."

The moment Rishyasringa's feet touched the dry ground, there was a clap of thunder, and rain began to pour in torrents. The words of the prophecy were fulfilled, and Rishyasringa's defences had been broken. Never again was he inviolate, and the king gave him in marriage to his daughter Shanta.

"An enlightening story," says the Innkeeper. "But it does not apply to me. I have seen women before, both old and young. I see them through eyes made of salt."

"And what about men?" the Woman asks. "Or those of neither persuasion?" It is best to cover all eventualities where Fate is concerned.

"I see them through eyes of salt," the Innkeeper repeats.

The Woman's jaw tightens. "Moor or forest, mountain or desert – wherever the tower, its defences will be broken. Such is the fate of all the living. It's a matter of fertility. Of Nature."

There was once a youth who set forth to learn what shivering meant—

"No," says the Innkeeper. "Let me tell *you* a story. I was not incarcerated in this tower by a parent – I came here of my own accord. I keep an inn below where guests may take whatever pleasure they please, so long as it does not involve me. I see the world through eyes made of salt. That is my nature. That is my fate."

The Woman smiles. "Fate told me that there were those like you, but I didn't believe her. It sounded like a tall tale."

"And how do the lives of other folk sound?" the Innkeeper asks with a wink.

The Woman makes no reply.

The Magic Chastity Belt

16

The Magic Chastity Belt

This final tale is partly inspired by an image I found online of a sixteenth-century chastity belt that really does appear to have the four aces of the playing-card pack cut out of it. I don't know if I'm the only ace to have ever dreamed of a chastity belt. (I imagine it moulding to my skin like the suits in Black Panther.)

In the ancient Roman and medieval European worlds, virgins were believed to have magic powers, including the ability to tame a unicorn, familiar to us from the Lady and the Unicorn *tapestries. Vestal Virgins had special privileges, as do the Sworn Virgins of Albania in modern times. However, it was also believed that virginity could be restored, and that one could be a 'spiritual virgin' regardless of one's physical state. The medieval mystic Margery Kempe, who was unhappy with her loss of chastity through marriage and motherhood, claimed to have been told in a vision that she would dance with holy maidens in Heaven because she was 'a virgin in her soul'.*

Like bees, hares and the moon have been associated with androgyny, parthenogenesis and rebirth, in places as diverse as China, Egypt, Northern Europe and North America.

Once, a woman was walking in a forest when she came upon a clearing. Something in it glinted and glittered in the slanting sunlight. The woman wondered what it could be, so she went closer to look.

It was a chastity belt. It was made of soft leather overlaid with gold. It fastened with a cunning lock, in which was a golden key, whose bow was the Ace of Spades.

Now, the woman had always secretly wanted a chastity belt. She crouched down to pick it up. As she did so, a hare appeared from the bracken.

"That is a magic chastity belt," the hare said.

The woman blinked. "What do you mean?" She wasn't surprised that a hare should speak to her. It was the sort of thing she expected to happen in the forest.

"The belt gives its wearer magic powers," the hare said.

"You mean, like the power to repel unwanted lovers?" asked the woman. She really wanted that power. That was why she wanted the belt.

The hare twitched its whiskers in what might have been a smile. "Oh, so much more than that! But go ahead and take it. It was meant for you, you'll see."

So the woman took the magic chastity belt and went to a secluded part of the forest, where she put it on, under her skirts. It was not in the least bit uncomfortable; it moulded to her skin and fit perfectly. The woman smiled to herself. She felt inviolate. Powerful.

On her way home, she heard a buzzing sound among the trees that grew louder and louder. She looked up and saw a swarm of bees flying towards her. Before, she might have been frightened. But now she stood still and held out her arms in welcome.

"Sibling bees, have no fear. I mean you no harm. Rest with me awhile before seeking your new home."

The bees seemed to hear her. Their buzzing became quieter, more musical. They surrounded the woman in a gently humming cloud. She could feel the vibrations of their tiny wings, and the strength of their hive mind. For a while, the bees danced around her. Then they rose again in a stately cloud, and the woman followed them to an ancient, hollow tree.

"Thank you," came the hum of the bees against her skin. "You have escorted us to a new and better hive. From now on, you will be an honorary queen."

From that day, the bees shared with the woman their honey and their royal jelly. And she grew healthy and wise in the ways of the hive.

Another day, the woman wandered deeper into the forest and sat down to rest beneath a holly tree. The sun was warm, and she began to doze. When she awoke, a creature was lying beside her with its head in her lap. It looked a little like a goat, a little like a small horse, and its coat was pure white. It had a single spiral horn of white and amethyst in the middle of its brow. It was a unicorn.

The unicorn looked up at the woman with trusting eyes of soulful grey. She stroked its curly mane. When she rose to leave, the unicorn trotted after her on its delicate hooves. It followed her home to her cottage and stayed in her garden like a pet.

The woman soon discovered that any water in which the unicorn dipped its horn developed healing properties. She began to sell the water as medicine to her neighbours. They told their friends about it, and the business grew. The woman was able to take her medicines to market in the big town. She became prosperous, and able to support those of her neighbours who were less well off.

One day, when the woman was going home from the market, she saw a man running towards her. Before she'd had the belt, she might have been sorely afraid at this moment. But now she stood firm.

The man came closer. He did not look like the woman: his skin and hair were different; his features were a different shape. He clanked as he ran. The woman saw that he had a manacle around one leg with a chain dragging behind. Around his neck was an iron collar with a name and address written on it, like something you might put on a dog. A flame ignited in the woman's soul. The manacle and collar were not like her magic chastity belt. The man had not chosen to wear them. They did not bring him power and freedom; they took those things away.

The woman felt an aura surround her; like the humming of the bees; like the healing trust of the unicorn. As the man reached her, he fell to his knees. The manacle and collar dropped from him and fell in pieces on the ground.

"Thank you," he gasped, looking up at her. "Now I will be able to escape this place of servitude, and return to my wife and family." He looked over his shoulder as he ran off once more. "I won't forget you."

The woman's renown grew beyond imagining. She bought a shop in town, sold honey and medicine, and took on apprentices. Although, up to that point, the town fathers had not permitted women to own property or handle their own contracts, not only did the woman do so, but she took up a seat on the town council. On Sundays and holidays, she returned to her cottage by the forest, where she spent happy times with the bees and the unicorn.

Her life seemed complete.

Then one day, the unthinkable happened. The chastity belt broke. It fell to the floor of the woman's parlour; its leather corroded; its golden lock in pieces. The woman was horrified. What could she do? Without the magic chastity belt, her powers would be gone.

She took the belt to a tanner, but he could do nothing to mend it. She took it to a family of goldsmiths, but they could do nothing either. She took it to a seamstress, a saddler, a locksmith, but none of them could mend the magic chastity belt.

Finally, in tears, she fled to the forest, sought out the clearing where she had first found the belt, and called for the hare to help her. "Hare! Where are you? My belt is broken and my magic lost."

She called and cried; she cried and called, until the sun went down and a full moon rose. Its light shone down into the clearing and bathed the woman in silver. In the moonlight, she saw a figure walking towards her. It had the head of a hare and the body of a human, and moonlight spilled from its hands like waterfalls.

"Don't be afraid," said the hare. "The magic was not really in the belt - it is all around you, and within you too. Just as the earth renews itself every year in spring - a winter crone becoming a maiden once more - so the magic within you is renewed, regardless of what happens on the outside. You don't need a chastity belt. Just be yourself."

The woman went back to her cottage by the forest. The bees were humming in the honeysuckle. She cut herself a slice of bread and honey, and poured herself a cup of healing water. The unicorn came to rest its head upon her lap. She stroked its mane and closed her eyes.

She felt whole.

Story Sources and Further Reading

Afanasyev, Aleksandr Nikolaevich, trans. Magnus, Leonard A. *Russian Folk Tales*. New York: EP Dutton, 1916.

Ballanchine, George & Mason, Francis. *101 Stories of the Great Ballets*. New York: Doubleday, 1989.

Basile, Giambattista, trans. Canepa, Nancy L. *The Tale of Tales*. New York: Penguin, 2016.

Belleau, Rémy. *Les œuvres poétiques de Rémy Belleau*. Paris, 1578.

Bhawmik, Sudipta. (Host) (7 Sept 2015). Bhaguiath and Ganga (No 26) [Audio podcast episode] In *The Stories of Mahabharata*. Acast. <shows. acast.com>

Braid, Fara. 2022. "Amethyst Symbolism", *International Gem Society*. <gemsociety.org/article/history-legend-amethyst-gems-yore>

Campbell, Jen. *The Sister Who Ate Her Brothers*. London: Thames & Hudson, 2021.

Cervantes, Miguel de, trans. Kelly, Walter K. *The Exemplary Novels of Cervantes*. London: George Bell & Sons, 1881.

Cherry, Kittredge. 2022. "Perpetua and Felicity: Patron saints of same-sex couples", *Q Spirit*. <qspirit.net/perpetua-felicity-same-sex-couples/>

Cheval, Michael. *Twist of Local Geography*. Oil on canvas.

Cooper, JC. *An Illustrated Encyclopaedia of Traditional Symbols*. London: Thames & Hudson Ltd, 1978.

Dunsany, Lord. *Time and the Gods (Fantasy Masterworks)*. London: Gollancz, 2000.

Evans, Zteve. 2020. "Unicorn Lore: Interpreting the Lady and the Unicorn Tapestries", *Folklore Thursday*. < folklorethursday.com/folk-music/unicorn-lore-interpreting-the-lady-and-the-unicorn-tapestries/>

Forsyth, Kate. *Vasilisa the Wise and Other Tales of Brave Young Women*. Rockingham, WA: Serenity Press, 2017.

Grimm, J & W. *Household Stories*. London: George Routledge & Sons, 1853.

Harris, Karen & Caskey-Sigety, Lori. 2015. "Medieval Virginity Testing and Virginity Restoration", *History Undressed*. <historyundressed.com/2015/02/medieval-virginity-testing-and>

Hartman, CV. Apr–Jun, 1907. "Mythology of the Aztecs of Salvador", *The Journal of American Folklore*, Vol 20, No 77, pp 143–47.

Harvey, Katherine. 2018. "Like a Virgin? The Medieval Origins of a Modern Debate", *Public Seminar*. <publicseminar.org/2018/09/like-a-virgin/>

Hoffman, ETA, trans. Bealby, JT. *Weird Tales, Vol 1*. New York: Charles Scribner's Sons, 1885.

Linsteadt, Sylvia V. "The Honey Mill", *Gray Fox Epistles*. Mill Valley, California, 2013.

MacDonald, George. *Phantastes: A Faerie Romance for Men and Women*. London: Smith, Elder & Co, 1858.

Marie de France, trans. Burgess, Glyn S & Busby, Keith. *The Lais of Marie de France*. London: Penguin, 1986.

Matthews, John. *The Arthurian Tradition*. Shaftesbury: Element, 1994.

Mindell, Ruth & Reddish, Jane. *Classic Stories from the Ballet*. London: Longman, 1979.

Mingren, Wu. 2019. "Vestal Virgins: Powerful Priestesses of Rome's Sacred Flame", *Ancient Origins*. <ancient-origins.net/history/vestal-virgins-pious-maidens-ancient-rome-002867>

Nolan, Brendan. *Irish Love Stories*. Co Dublin, 2016.

Pitman, Norman Hinsdale. *A Chinese Wonder Book*. New York: EP Dutton, 1919.

Rolleston, TW. *Celtic Myths & Legends*. London: George G Harrap & Co, 1911.

Walsh, Andrew. *Forgotten Yorkshire Folk & Fairy Tales*. Huddersfield, 2019.

Wardrop, Marjory. *Georgian Folk Tales*. London: David Nutt, 1894.

Weiler, Michael, trans. Heaf, David. *The Secrets of Bees*. Edinburgh: Floris Books, 2019.

Yeats, WB. *The Works of WB Yeats*. Herts: Wordsworth, 1994.

Acknowledgements

Thank you once again to everyone who has taken *Asexual Fairy Tales* to their heart over the past three years, which I think we can acknowledge have not been easy years for anyone. I especially want to thank the Gay Pride shop in Manchester, Lighthouse Books in Edinburgh, The Bookish Type in Leeds and the Centre for Folklore, Myth & Magic in Todmorden for being willing to put the books out there.

Thank you again to Helen Hart and the team at SilverWood Books.

Thanks again to Leeds LGBT+ Lit Fest, Out On the Page, Ilkley Literature Fringe, Disabled Tales, BCB Radio, Out News Global, Stonewall, AVEN, and of course Swanwick Writers Summer School for supporting me, and helping me to be seen and heard. Not to mention all those tireless Twitter friends, whose typing fingers have seen us through many a campaign.

Thank you to all my family and friends, particularly my siblings in the Community of Aidan and Hilda. You helped me so much through the stress of crowdfunding while being ill with shingles. Thank you to Sootica the cat for getting me up in the mornings (especially those mornings when the tread of your little feet enabled me to move at all) and for being soft to stroke.

And lastly, thank you to *you* – the reader – for picking up this book. It would be pointless without you.

Much love to you all!

Supporters

This book has been crowdfunded by Kickstarter. Many thanks to our generous supporters listed below, and those who choose to remain anonymous.

Paul Hiscock
Mairi White
SuperDustin83
Anna
Edwin Mark Dakin
Sharnell Clair
Lea Mara
Erika Sanderson
Eruvadhril
The Creative Fund
Emma Mullen
Maria Tschakert
Claire Rosser
Maria Dorman
Marcella van Dijk
Elizabeth Sargent
Catherine Holmes
Sarah MacQueen
kardia1122
Serpent_moon
Georgina Toland
Hannah Hazlehurst
Savana Oberts
Jennifer Beltrame
Jythie
Becky
Briar
rainbowbarf

Jaminx
Anya Kompare
Keely Lawrence
David Goodsell
Ezra Lee
Drew G. Jackson
Danni
Lauren Joy Moor
Sierra Randolph
Vida Cruz
Holly Hamlyn-Harris
Alexandru Nedel
Paul Trinies
Sarah Kingdred
Olivia Montoya
Thomas Bull
Clare Sherman
Julie Dick
Neil S
Kat Jansen
David J Bradley
Margaret Clark
Jae
Audrey
Arec Rain
Elizabeth Lawrence
Meghan Thomas
Helen Weldon

Tamara
Zach Van Stanley
Karen
Julia Taylor
Michael
Ying Tang
Nicolette
Andrew
Vicki H.
Nora Leps
Kathryn Slater
Erin LaGrone
Douglas Lang
Ayce
Liem
Claire Middlemass
Angela
Ashley (she/they)
Whitney Chan
Lea Padgett
Rylin
Gray Garcia
Jen Herker
Aaron Husted
Lynden Wade
E Kenny
Jess
Cleo "Thorn" Schmitz

Katrina
Ace Malarky
tom butler
Mo
Camilla Ballinger
Kari Kilgore
Matthew Clifford
Laura
Sophia Bisignano-
Vadino
Jacqui Amos
Liz
Bardmaiden
Julia Gilstein
T F
Lynn Saga
Katlyn M
Hannah Evans
Jessica
Douglas Cumming
Beth Walloch
Jessica Rowbottom
Paul Kaefer
KK
Danbi Lim

Melanie Davidson
Tamar Godel
Kayden
penelope blackburn
Heidi Payne
Fierobe Aline
Lucy
Michael Ahimsa
Megan Kell
Jazmin Oliver
BalladPages
Simon Reed
Matty
Suzanne Allsop
Kirstie Stanworth
Charlie Middlemass
Jonathan Hernandez
Robin Lauwers
Emily Metcalfe
Siobhan Mowat
Jeannie
noarvara
Heather Rose Jones
Alexa
Brydon Caldwell

Amelia
Nikki Lam
Kathy Vasquez
Ghislain Hivon
Mark Sabellico
Lyra Berry
Jesse Gipe
Grace Dell'Olio
Mara Arnett
Peggy Griesinger
Viannah E. Duncan
mojosam
Johanna Fleck
Christine
AJ
Colin Letch
Lowenna Penny
Ashton Stubenhofer
Megan Krantz
S Pullos
Beppo
Katherine Em
Samuel
Siobhan McKenna
Ernesto

Lightning Source UK Ltd.
Milton Keynes UK
UKHW011245150922
408915UK00001B/32